MUSIC FOR THE OFF-KEY

TWELVE MACABRE SHORT STORIES

ALSO BY COURTTIA NEWLAND

The Scholar (1997)
Society Within (1999)
Snakeskin (2002)
The Dying Wish (2006)

Co-edited:
IC: 3 (2000)
Tell Tales: The Anthology of Short Stories: Vols. 1 & 2 (2005)

COURTTIA NEWLAND

MUSIC FOR THE OFF-KEY

TWELVE MACABRE SHORT STORIES

To
Nikki

One Love!

Courttia Newland

PEEPAL TREE

First published in Great Britain in 2006
Peepal Tree Press Ltd
17 King's Avenue
Leeds LS6 1QS
UK

ISBN 13: 9781845230401

Peepal Tree gratefully acknowledges Arts Council support

ACKNOWLEDGEMENTS

Praises to the Most High for giving me strength, belief and self-determination, and the spirits of my ancestors for guiding my way.

Big respect to all the people who supported me during the writing of these stories. Yin, who looked after me when no one else would – I'll never forget that. Mum, my rock, Sledge for keeping me grounded, Jules for the laughter, Deb, Liz, Greg and Jim for the belief in my work (Jim, our musical chats always remind me where I'm coming from!). Thanks to Liam Gallimore Wells for always being there, and Paul Beasley at 57 Productions for always getting me there! Kadija, it's a blessing to work with you again sis! Let's run that extra mile! Thanks to Dorothea Smartt for your smile of encouragement at readings, and Nii Parkes for all your kind words! Hey to Alex Harvey, hope all is good on your side of the world... To Anissa-Jane, thanks for my favourite book cover, you make magic with colours... Big up each and every one of the Tell Tales crew, keep writing those shorts and good luck those of you with novel deals! Sharmila, you're my best friend! Thanks for keeping the faith!

One Love to all of the publishers/editors who commissioned or printed my stories in the past. Love to Jeremy and Hannah at Peepal Tree Press for having guts when so many others fell short. I can't forget Richard Beswick, who never forgot me. Lots of love goes out to Eugenie Furniss, the best agent in the world!

RIP to my uncle Winston Denny who taught me that the world isn't always fair, but it's usually just.

For Marlene Denny

CONTENTS

'These can't be the only notes in the world. There have to be other notes someplace, in some dimension, between the cracks of the piano keys...'

Marvin Gaye

SUICIDE NOTE

Hot water cascaded from shiny metal taps, to foam, bubble and churn in the bath. Steam rose, swirled, made the air around him hot and moist, heightening his feeling of sensuality, caressing his pores. Welling stuck out his tongue and felt the tiny water particles landing. He closed his eyes and arched his head back, giving in to the moment, relishing the moisture's light touch on his body, like a thousand lips kissing him all over.

He ran his hands over himself. Over his meaty chest, flat stomach, then down to his penis. Fingers splayed, he stroked the coarse and curly pubic hair, rubbing his balls, moving along the hard, veined ridges of his member until he reached the head. He pulled his uncircumcised foreskin back as far as he could. His fingers curled into a fist, sliding his foreskin over the head; it disappeared, returned as he repeated his actions. Slow at first, then more rapid. Soon his fist was a blur, his breathing laboured.

The water had risen too high. He forced himself to stop and shut off the taps. For a moment Welling stared at the steaming water as if it were a mirror and he could see some reflection of himself within its depths. His chest still rose and fell. He gripped the bath sides and climbed in.

Soap, flannel, pumice stone, razor blade. They were all there, sitting at the side of the tub. He picked up the soap and flannel, washing himself methodically, making sure every crevice and pore was clean. When he was satisfied, the pumice stone had its turn, and he scrubbed at the hard bits of flesh on his toes and heels. Soon he'd smoothed them down. He put back the grey piece of volcanic rock, next to the soap and flannel.

Now for the razor blade.

He lay back as far as he could, knees in the air; toes just below the twin taps. The blade between the fingers of his right hand glinted like a devilish eye. He raised his left arm out of the water, staring in wonder at the network of veins, arteries and tendons. He'd always been veiny. Whenever his doctor wanted a sample of blood, they never needed to use a garrotte, his veins were so obvious. He flexed his fingers. The tendons moved in compliance, like pulleys. He smiled.

It was time.

Breathing lightly, he moved his right hand closer to his left. If he'd had an extra hand, it would have been holding his penis; he was excited, and his excitement grew the closer the blade got to skin. When the sharp corner touched his wrist he gasped with pent up tension; then brought the blade across in one swift movement. For a moment there was nothing. Then the skin went pale and blood came rushing to the surface. Quickly, he did the same to his right wrist, then put both wrists in the tub and lay back. His hardened penis protruded from the water as though watching the proceedings.

After fifteen minutes he knew it wasn't working.

The bath was getting cold and his blood wasn't filling the tub. There was a little bit of pink water where his arms were resting, but apart from that, nothing to mark what he'd done. He lifted them up, inspecting the slashes on each wrist. Wounds as fatal as paper cuts adorned them. They'd stopped bleeding, and were starting to sting. His penis had sunk back beneath the water, bored by the display.

He couldn't do it. As much as he wanted to, he simply couldn't do it. He didn't know if it was because of his Catholic upbringing or his love of pain, but every time that he tried it just wouldn't work. Welling wanted to die. Had long wanted it. But every quest to meet his end became another chance to explore his sexuality, rather than a real attempt at death. It had to happen before he went too far. Last week only proved him right. He didn't deserve to live, but loved himself too much to do the necessary thing.

That was him. Selfish to the last.

He'd known he was sick long before last week; it was too obvious to miss. But his time with Corelle was like a sedative. She made him forget, made him docile, made him believe he was normal.

With Suzanne, he knew he couldn't kid himself. He'd been sitting in a Soho coffee shop, his favourite prowling ground. He loved the place; the dank staircases, neon lights, black rubber boots, whips and chains. He could stroll from street to street, his face blank, his mind whirring. He could enter the shops, staircases and nobody cared.

The girl appeared on the opposite corner of the street. He paused mid-sip, the rim of his coffee mug lightly touching his lower lip. Her skin was darker than ink. She was tall, mature, dignified. Her hair was tied back, resting loosely against her neck. A broad red bag packed with books and girlie fanzines hung from her shoulder. Her grey school skirt was short, exposing smooth, curved legs to his gaze.

She was exquisite.

He watched as she talked with a gathering of school friends. She was easily the tallest of the group, the most physically mature, the ringleader – judging by the other girls' actions which, through the window of the bar, proved as entertaining as a mime show. They laughed and gossiped, mini-caricatures of grown women, evidently loud and raucous, but oblivious to the glances of Soho passers-by. Fifteen minutes later she was still there, entrancing him with the unconscious fluidity of her girlhood. She was aware of her growing body, but her awareness was somehow detached – the way she played with her ponytail, ran an absent hand along her thigh, licked her lips before she spoke: all constant accompaniments to words he could not hear. After a further twenty minutes, by his watch, the group said their reluctant goodbyes and went off in different directions. Suzanne (although he didn't know that was her name yet) shouldered her bag and walked right past his window seat. She was alone. He downed the cold coffee he'd been nursing and rapidly left the shop.

At this point, as he'd walked behind the girl, Welling knew that he was crossing a forbidden boundary. Such thoughts were rare, mostly confined to the early morning hours alone in bed. She was a schoolgirl. Little older than fifteen, possibly as young as twelve.

As for him... He was pushing forty, his mind full of lurid scenarios involving a girl who could almost be his daughter. Forty years old, filled with a sickness he couldn't control. Harbouring feelings that leaked down his inside thigh as he walked.

She strode through the crowd of commuters with a confidence that he found all the more enticing. His misgivings disappeared. Sometimes, somehow, this was the most exciting part. When they didn't know him, hadn't met him, and were open to his unshielded gaze. He cast his eyes over calves that tensed athletically as she walked. Up the backs of her thighs, which did the same. Further upward, to the hemline of her brief skirt, tightening over rounded cheeks that rolled left, right, left... He grew harder at the sight, his want all-consuming. He walked faster, caught her up, and placed a hand just above her elbow. Startled, she turned around to face him.

He knew he'd be all right when she took in his features, her eyebrows raised in a silent question.

'Oh...' he stuttered. 'I thought –'

She continued to stare, amused by his seeming discomfort.

'I thought –' he continued. The timing had to be right. 'Are you – you're a singer aren't you?'

She put her hands on curving hips with a coy smile, displaying perfect white teeth. He was stunned. She was even more gorgeous close up.

'Why, do I look like a singer?'

'You're that girl from that R&B group ain' you? 411 or suttin' like that. You sing the lead, right?'

She giggled and shook her head.

'Everybody says that, says I look like her. It ain' me though. I can sing but I ain' in a group yet.'

They looked each other over. Welling could see that she was sizing him up. Some teenage girls loved the fact that older men were interested in them, but at the end of the day, you couldn't look *too* old. A bit wrinkly around the eyes and mouth, a few grey hairs plucked out over the last few months, but he jogged, worked out, and ate well, so he knew he looked more than adequate. Suzanne seemed to agree. She was looking him boldly in the eye, closing the space between them until there was barely any left. Although she was tall for her age, she still had to look up to achieve this task. Sweat burst out on his forehead as warm breath caressed his chin.

'Why, are you a music manager or suttin'?'

'Nah… I'm an artist. I paint pictures and I think you're quite beautiful. I'd like to paint your portrait. Please.'

She giggled again, playing coy, stepping from foot to foot before gazing back up at him.

'Thank you,' she breathed, mouth open, lips glistening from apricot balm, the odour surrounding her like an aura. Her eyes were dark and slanted, blinking at him. She was standing so close he could see his reflection in them.

It was easy as that.

Over the next few weeks, Suzanne became a regular visitor to his West London tower-block home, which doubled as his studio. He took his time painting her, using pencils to sketch an outline, then expensive oils to colour and define her further. Suzanne was quick-witted and feisty. She was a willing model, sitting in a relaxed and natural manner, eagerly obeying his commands to turn and hold still. They talked as he worked, and got to know each other's minds as he familiarised himself with her body, learning more with each line he painted. The once a week meeting grew into twice, then three times. Sessions became longer, stretching far into the night. On these occasions, he'd call for a cab to drive the girl to her Harlesden home; and though he wondered what she told her parents, he never dared to ask for fear of the answer. He knew she hadn't told her friends about him, for when they called on her mobile she was furtive and vague about her whereabouts.

They moved from smiles to touching. She was assured and confident, very mature. He began to think that Corelle's absence was a good thing.

During one late night session, an unusual silence had fallen between them, comfortable despite its length. Welling was concentrated on the painting, on her head and shoulders, clear eyes, high cheekbones, baby-smooth skin. Frowning, he flicked his paintbrush over the cleft of the painted Suzanne's chin, stood back and thought for a second, comparing his subject with her likeness.

Suzanne was sitting with a hand against her head, teeth clenched and wincing with pain. The glass of Holstein Pils she'd asked for when she arrived was untouched. His concern was instant.

'You OK?'

Suzanne looked up, morose. 'I got a headache. It's killin' me man.'

'I got some painkillers in the bathroom if you want 'em.'

'Yeah, all right. Thanks.'

She got to her feet, walking past him and out into the bathroom. He continued to paint a little longer, then gave up and took another few steps back. The painting was looking very good. He was so obviously inspired it frightened him – as if here, with Suzanne, he'd crossed some boundary never to return. Welling sighed and placed his brush in a pot of water by the easel, then stared through the window at the expanse of lights and streets.

Maybe things *were* getting too deep. He was supposed to be trying to stop, trying to change the way he looked at the world. Corelle leaving him had been a test he'd been sure he could pass – before he'd seen Suzanne. He'd thought he was stronger than that.

It was going to happen and there was nothing he could do about it.

Welling sat staring into the night for almost half an hour before he realised Suzanne hadn't returned. He found her sitting on the edge of the bath, her tears silent yet passionate, forced into her hands. A quick glance around the bathroom informed him of the cause – the open cabinet, with its contents of deodorants, painkillers, Listerine, and an open box of Corelle's tampons. He looked from the open cabinet to the girl. Gently, he perched beside Suzanne on the bath rim, reaching out a hand.

'Suzanne, don't get like that–'

'I thought you said you was single!' she blubbered, pushing him away with a wet hand. He slid closer to the taps and stayed where she'd pushed him, his reply calm.

'I am single…'

'Then what's that!'

She pointed at the offending blue box.

14

'That's my ex-girlfriend's. She hasn't lived here for three months.'

Actually, it was only one month, but telling her that wouldn't make her feel any better. Suzanne had long been hiding her real feelings from him, though she could flirt with the best of them. They'd hugged, kissed and she'd even massaged him once (clothes on), yet throughout she'd kept a healthy distance between them. All at once, he was faced with what he'd been fantasising about. As if he'd called it into being, here was his final test.

Welling looked over her curves and knew he'd failed.

'You must think I'm jus' a stoopid little kid,' Suzanne was complaining through her haze of tears. 'All my friends told me you'd be like dis, and they was right.'

'Don't say that.' He took her hand. She allowed this contact, still refusing to hold his gaze. 'If I did have a girlfriend, don't you think you would have seen her here? After all, you've bin here four or five times a week, the past four weeks. If my ex *was* living here, you would've met her by now, don't you reckon?'

'I've only bin 'ere three times a week,' she replied, haughty now.

He laughed, unable to stop himself touching her hair. Suzanne stiffened, but still defied his attention, eyes latched to the aqua-blue tiled walls. His fingers strayed from her hair, to her cheekbones, then her lips, caressing their softness. Suzanne closed her eyes, leant her head back, and let her dark-tinged lips fall open, tongue exploring the roughened ridges of his fingers. Surprised, he wondered if this was the way she sucked ice poles on her way home from school – and while he was shocked at the thought, he was also aroused – undeniably aroused. He slid his way along the bath, moving closer to the girl, who turned to him blindly, lips parted, eyes still closed.

Her kiss began clothed in innocence, but was stripped bare until her passion was exposed in the dim light of the room. Her youthful probing was confident, but her imitations of his lust betrayed how much she had yet to learn. Feeling her inexperience and knowing that there was still time to find his way back, Welling tried to stop. He backed away from her, opened his eyes. Looking at Suzanne's smooth, dark face, free of wrinkles and marked only by the signs of adolescent transition, it was impossible to deny what she really was. The vision caught him for a moment. Long braided ponytail, cobalt mascara, fruit-scented body spray. Her school shirt, its collar curled and faded by numerous washings. She was a young, virtually untouched girl. Losing herself in the moment, Suzanne moved forwards, eyes still closed, blind to Welling's tiny moment of indecision, oblivious to his doubt. While he watched, too horrified by what he'd become to stop her, Suzanne forced her tongue back inside his mouth. A warm hand moved beneath his clothes; small fingers found his nipple, beginning to stroke and pinch. He kissed her in return, trying to tell himself he was only doing it to save her from rejection. Then, as she responded, his thoughts were only on how good she smelt, her taste, her heat. He parted her legs with the same fingers that had been pressed between her lips – although now they squeezed and kneaded warm thighs, sure in their quest, ceaseless in their journey. She opened her legs wider to ease his passage. He traced the hemline of her knickers, rubbed the fleshy mound. She rested one foot up on the toilet bowl. He moved the knickers to one side, knowing he'd found what he sought when Suzanne cried out – a keening exhalation of breath that had her clutching his shoulder. She was tight, wet, her pleasure dampening her inner thighs. He rubbed harder as she became moister, deeper as her hips writhed in pleasure, faster as she sucked hard on his tongue.

He felt orgasm flood her body and knew Suzanne was his. She kissed him soulfully and he lifted her into his bedroom.

Their relationship took a new turn. She became more intense and demanding. Though he'd wanted her to fall for him, Welling hadn't been able to foresee exactly how hard she'd hit the ground. Within two months, the happy-go-lucky, sassy young thing had changed into a brooding, paranoid girlfriend, ever watchful of her man. Admittedly, he hadn't handled the transition well. He stopped calling so often, snapped at her when she complained about his lack of attention, openly spoke of other women. Suzanne came out fighting. She screamed at him, smashed plates in fury, and when all of this went unheeded, she committed the ultimate sin – destroying his painting of her, first by using his oils to deface it, then grabbing a knife from the kitchen and puncturing it in several places. All of this because a female friend had rung the flat, asking Suzanne if Welling was ready to paint her. He'd been out at the shops when it happened. On his return, the sight of the torn canvas, as thin and fragile as human skin, ignited his anger in a way that she'd never seen. He hit her, many times, until she was a bawling heap on his studio floor, mouth and nose streaming with blood. He noted the thick, glassy redness for a moment before shock rolled in. Then it was: 'Suzanne, I'm so sorry, Suzanne please forgive me...'

She stared up at him in disbelief, allowing herself to be helped to her feet, allowing him to move her to a chair, sit her down, run into the bathroom for the First Aid kit. When he returned, the seat was empty apart from a scrap of paper that shuddered from the breeze of an open window as though alive and feeling the cold. First Aid kit in hand, he picked up the paper with a heavy heart. Two words were scrawled with what looked like one of his 4HB pencils – two words, no more, no less.

I'm pregnant.

He never saw her again.

Fate eventually led him to the BT telephone box, on that windy Soho street where he'd first seen her. He took his failed suicide attempt as a sign that he should force some contact with Suzanne, if only for the sake of his child. Corelle's face appeared whenever he closed his eyes, damning him to hell, telling him that he'd never changed, that he'd failed again; only this time it was much, much worse. When he tired of Suzanne's repeated answer phone message, he took to sitting in the coffee shop where he'd first laid eyes on her – day in, day out, with no reprieve or success. He drank so many cappuccinos his nights were as lengthy as his days and his eyes grew thick dark rings.

Prowling the dingy side streets was tiring. He saw many schoolgirls in those lonely days; none of them was Suzanne.

Then one afternoon, out of the corner of his eye, Welling saw her – that head high, confident walk and swinging black ponytail. He jumped out of his seat, pushed past an elderly couple just entering the shop and ran recklessly after her. When he reached the corner of the block, he'd lost her. He swore in frustration, startling suits and shoppers alike. Looking from side to side, he saw the BT telephone box standing like a beacon – a signal pulsing for him alone.

An idea took root. If she was in Soho, her mobile might be on. He could call and get her to meet him. He could make amends.

He crossed the road and fairly flew into the box, inserting his change and dialling as fast as he could; then waited, breath held deep in his lungs. Two beats and nothing. Four, and still the empty static of an electronic world. Five, and he received the deafening three tones that indicated a disconnected line. He slumped against the glass of the box in defeat. Suzanne's number had been the only real link he'd had. If that was gone it meant that he'd surely lost her. Agony for his unseen child – his *only* child – consumed him. He sobbed, looking up at the ceiling as if in silent protest to the Most High.

There was a card on that ceiling. Fluorescent pink, stuck with Blu Tack and hanging like a ripe fruit, demanding to be picked. At first he mistook it for a prostitute's calling card and looked back down at his feet. He closed his eyes. The words he'd seen for a tenth of a second flashed in his mind. Shocked, in one fluid movement, he looked back up, and reached. He held the card close. He hadn't been mistaken. It said what he had seen.

SUICIDE NOTE
0208 743 2920

The words kept replaying in his head. Suicide Note. What did that mean? Could he believe it was what he thought? That, at the very moment when hope had seemed useless, there was a glimmer of light?

He didn't know the answer to any of those questions, but he dialled the number on that pink card all the same.

The office was on the tenth floor of an office block in Shepherd's Bush. The block seemed to house myriad small businesses in a rabbit warren of passages and doors. The receptionist on the other end of the phone line had given him an address and door number, both of which he'd scribbled onto the back of the pink card. When he reached room D-474, he stopped and looked at the card, then back at the door. It was a plain, unpainted wood-brown colour, devoid even of varnish, bearing only two letters – S.N. Welling knocked once, entering when requested.

The reception area was kitted out in more wood-brown colours – pine, mahogany, oak, beech. The woman he assumed had spoken to him on the phone got to her feet and crossed the room to greet him, arm outstretched.

'Mr. Welling?'

'Yes…'

'Glad you could make it!'

She was an Asian beauty with features close to perfection, long black hair, and a calm enthusiasm that surprised, yet comforted him. He saw that she had one grey eye and one brown, which gave her face the feline look of a tiger. *She'd be amazing to paint*, he told himself. Welling hadn't touched his paintbrush since he'd hit Suzanne, which seemed like years ago. He wanted to ask the receptionist to pose for him, but settled for shaking her hand.

'Ms. Grantham has just finished with another client – you can go right through.' Her voice, warm and soft, guided him towards another doorway. He was jarred by the fact that this door, unlike any of the others in the office, was painted a glossy black, dark enough to see his reflection. A gold plaque told him that this was the office of Toby Grantham, Managing Director.

He was suddenly very afraid.

'Thank you.'

It seemed to take forever to reach the door, but before he knew it he was there. He knocked. A muffled voice called for him to enter.

This office had a colour scheme that matched the reception, though black and gold was mixed in amongst the wood panels. A huge bay window provided a panoramic view of London; in front of it was a large black and gold desk. Sitting behind the desk, with her back to the window, was a middle-aged white woman, full of smiles and dressed in an attractive lime-green suit. She got to her feet, her suit moulding itself to the curves of her body – he noticed that she was quite sexy; in a mature, dignified way. A straight,

19

pointed nose, chiselled jaw, ocean-blue eyes. Where the receptionist's eyes were friendly, Grantham's showed nothing but curiosity. He took her smooth, baby-soft hand within his own.

'Mr. Welling...'

'Yes, that's right.'

'I'm Toby Grantham, Managing Director of Suicide Note. Sit down, make yourself comfortable. Would you like tea, coffee, orange juice?'

'Coffee please.'

He sat on the expansive black leather seat and looked around the office while Grantham ordered their drinks through the intercom. Books lined the wall, on shelves that looked as though they were straining under their weight. Most seemed like hardback nonfiction, apart from one sitting on the desk in front of him. *The Five Gates of Hell*, by Rupert Thomson. He frowned, leaning closer to inspect the spine – yes, he knew it; this was a book he'd read. It was about a town that thrived on the business of funerals and death. He wondered if Grantham had read it yet.

'Coffee's on the way,' she told him, a tiny smile at the corner of her lips. She motioned at the book. 'Have you read it?'

'Yes, I have.'

'Good?'

'Not bad. Did you like it?'

'I did.' She beamed a perfect smile over the desk at him. 'You could say it was right up my street.'

Welling smiled vaguely. Any words he might have voiced died in his throat. She was watching him like an anxious baker waiting for bread to rise.

'Where did you come from?'

'The West End. Soho,' he replied, cursing himself for getting specific. 'I saw your card in one of the phone boxes.'

The woman smiled at him. 'That's great, really great.'

There was a long silence, in which he looked everywhere but at her, and she appraised him openly. The receptionist knocked, put the drinks on the desk, and exited without a word. The rich smell of fresh coffee filled the room. He reached for the mug as if it were a lifeline.

'So, Mr. Welling... How can we help you?'

Welling started at the beginning – when he first discovered his passion for young girls, working up to the point where he'd met Suzanne. He was deeply embarrassed, especially having to say these things to a woman, but Toby Grantham's encouraging nods urged him on; pretty soon he'd lost himself in the telling of the story. By the time he got to his failed suicide attempt, he was talking faster, passionately even, his penis a hard rod inside his jeans. He shifted a little, then stuttered to a halt, realising where he was once more.

'It's OK, Mr. Welling, you don't have to say any more. Let me explain what Suicide Note is about.'

He nodded and sipped at his cooling coffee.

'Suicide Note was founded by my father in 1980; he very sadly passed away in '92. The idea came from that old argument about euthanasia – you know, if a man or woman wants to take their life, is it right for someone to help them? My father thought the laws concerning this type of thing were antiquated, completely irrelevant in some cases – such as yours. He founded this company to find a humane way to provide such a service, and allow decent people the dignity of choice.

'Suicide Note works like this. We have an in-house psychiatrist who looks you over mentally, and a doctor to check the physical side of things. They're basically making sure you're of sound body and mind. When you've been passed and you're still sure you want to go through with things, you sign a contract with us to that effect, which bonds you to Suicide. Think very carefully before you make that decision, Mr. Welling – you can't turn the clock back once you've signed. We send all the papers to outside contractors after that. Once they receive your papers, you can't change things. They finish the job within two weeks.'

Finish the job. He gulped back the sudden lump in his throat.

'You said outside contractors – does that mean hit men?'

Grantham made a disgusted face.

'No – not hit men at all, Mr. Welling; they're too humane to be called anything like that. Our staff are made up of professionals, ex-doctors and the like. There are certainly no guns or other weapons involved – death is usually achieved painlessly by lethal injection or a pill of some kind.'

She smiled again when she said that, then sat back and watched his reaction. Welling blinked, rubbing at his head. When he closed his eyes, he saw Suzanne lying on his studio floor, mouth and nose bleeding, hands on her lower stomach. He wanted to cry out to Grantham, tell her he'd never meant the girl any harm; he only wanted to love her, but she'd destroyed his art, and he'd reacted instinctively to that. It took another quick moment, but thinking back over all the young girls he'd seduced helped him put that particular episode into perspective. Suzanne, truth be told, wasn't the first he'd hit. Melanie had been sleeping with a boy from her school. Nadine had caught him going out of the house with Corelle. Tashee had made a disparaging comment about his art one evening. When he looked at his back catalogue, things were worse than he'd ever been able to admit.

Now this woman and her company were offering him the chance to accept what he was and make a decision about how to deal with it. He had to grab the lifeline. Either that, or drown in his own shit, taking every innocent girl he was destined to meet in the future with him.

Grantham waited before speaking. When she did, there was no pressure, no goading in her voice. Instead, it was tinged with curiosity and gentle caring. He found himself eased by her pleasant tone.

'What do you think?'

Welling looked up.

'Do it,' he whispered to the woman. 'Do it.'

So they did.

He saw the physical doctor first, then the head doctor. When both were finished, he sat in the reception area reading a magazine, vainly attempting not to stare at the receptionist's legs. It took forty-five minutes, but he was eventually called back into Grantham's office, where he sat rubbing his sweaty palms against his thighs. He'd passed – and was legally certified to be in perfect physical and mental health. His contract, a piece of A4 paper the exact shade of Grantham's ocean-blue eyes, sat on the desk in front of him, his full name neatly typed at the top. Grantham nodded and motioned for him to look it over. He took the

contract and scanned the words, blurred vision and legal termi-
nology making it hard to read.

> *P. H. Welling hereafter to be known as (THE CLIENT),*
> *being of sound mind and body, grants Suicide Note, hereafter*
> *to be known as (THE COMPANY) the divine right to*
> *perform an act of artificial suicide on behalf of THE CLIENT*
> *within two weeks, beginning from the date specified below…*

15th June 2005

There was more, but none of the rest made any difference. He
had to stop himself before he seriously hurt one of the girls who
so innocently trusted in him. He signed his name at the bottom
of the contract, then handed it over to Grantham with a tiny
portion of relief lodged in his heart.

He arrived at the foyer of his tower block about three hours later.
After leaving Shepherd's Bush, he'd found himself travelling
back to central London – not Soho, but the South Bank – packed
with as many tourists, but calmer, sedated, more serene. He
walked the Thames, along a pathway that took him past Tower
Bridge, London Bridge and others. Tired, he took a taxi home,
thinking that he might as well spend the money.

His thoughts whirled like kites caught by the strength of a
blustery wind. No more would he watch London lights after
nightfall. No more would he marvel at female forms that graced
grimy streets. No late-night Garage pirate stations, hot summers
lazing in Hyde Park, or Sunday dinners with *Eastenders* on TV. It
was all denied him now, never to be given back. His copy of the
ocean-blue contract burned a hole through his inside pocket; he
knew why he'd signed, but the sight of his familiar scrawl on that
paper had created a void he could never have imagined and
wouldn't wish on an enemy.

Welling was scared to die.

He stepped blindly through the foyer and over to a trio of lifts,
pressing the call button almost in a trance. His hand was trembling. He looked at it, entranced by its gyrations, which were

completely out of his control. The lift's bell *pinged* and the metal doors opened. He stepped inside.

'Paul…' came a hesitant voice behind him.

It's her, the voice inside him croaked in a whisper. He turned, his heart leaping, almost unable to believe. But it was true. Corelle stood there, beautiful hazel eyes narrowed in concern. She'd cut her hair; it curled in a short bob around her head, framing her small face like opening and closing brackets. The style suited her. She was even more stunning than before.

'I came earlier, but you weren't home, so I waited… Do you mind?'

He shook his head, mute. If he spoke… If he spoke, it would all come tumbling out – everything he'd done, every backward step.

'It's been so long. I missed you Paul… I couldn't do it any longer. I forgive you. D'you get me? It doesn't matter any more, I forgive you.'

Welling gaped at her, unable to voice his emotions – unable to admit he'd been convinced he'd never see her again. Too many things had happened, too many girls; he'd messed up too many times… Surely he didn't deserve her back in his life. Corelle was one in a million, everybody said as much – she managed to touch everyone she came in contact with. She had one of those person- alities – the kind who was loved by all. A woman like Corelle was almost too good to exist in a world as corrupt as the one he inhabited.

Maybe he wasn't good enough, but without her he was nothing. He had proved that beyond any doubt. He needed her around him, now more than ever. Whether he'd tell her about Suzanne, or the subsequent fall out from that latest incident, was another, deeper matter.

'I'm… glad you came back… I missed you,' he stumbled, eyes cast down on the lift floor. She lifted his head with a light finger – he relishing her touch – and stared into his eyes. They hugged tight. She turned and pressed the button for his floor, guiding him, taking control.

Luck and love had visited him in one fell swoop – he immersed himself in both, secure in the feeling. On that first night, they made up with a combination of Indian takeaway, bottles of beer and fierce lovemaking, just as they'd done many times before, all those months ago. It was good to get back into the world he knew, the woman he knew – his rightful space in time. They lay in bed for almost two days, catching up on all the things they'd experienced while apart, or reliving special moments they'd shared. Corelle had given up her nursing job and found work as an assistant to a well-known artist, attempting to gain experience by working with someone else. The sketches she showed him were of such a high standard he wondered how close the relationship had been – but refrained from asking, his fear of knowledge defeating him once again. Instead, he told her of pictures he'd created in her absence, showing her abstract paintings of buildings, the woman who lived four floors down – other things that had nothing to do with Suzanne, or the work he'd done with her. The painting of the young girl was stashed safely at the bottom of a cupboard in his bedroom – gone, but not forgotten. His pact with Suicide Note was treated in much the same fashion; pushed into a distant corner of his mind, unwanted though never completely discarded.

On their fourth morning together, he awoke around five am to find Corelle snoring beside him, low down on the mattress, arms clasping her head. He slipped from beneath the duvet, padded across the room and made up a selection of brushes. Setting up his paints, palette, and easel next to the bed, he sketched with total abandon, brow furrowed in concentration. If she turned or rolled over, he simply moved to the opposite side of the bed, continuing where he'd left off. It took several hours, but what he created was a bizarre mixture of real and surreal; a sleeping beauty crafted in Corelle's likeness, lying on a bed made up of the grimy London streets he'd reminisced about the night he'd signed that ocean-blue contract. Behind her was the London skyline at night, twinned with that of another country – Africa or the West Indies, (he wasn't quite sure yet) – made up of huge trees, an orange/russet sun peeking out from behind mountains. By the time she opened her eyes he'd sketched it all, and had painted most of the background, calling his new piece *Sidewalk Princess*. Corelle laughed when she saw what he'd done; then wrapped her limbs around him, pulling him back to bed.

The following few days relived the blissful honeymoon period they'd enjoyed at the beginning of their relationship. They shopped, ate out, watched movies, went raving and found each other once more. He was in love with Corelle all over again, finding the current deeper and stronger, moving him along at a speed that was relentless. At night, he found his muse again and again, painting pictures while she slept.

It was only at the end of the first week, when Corelle went back to work, that he gave Suicide Note any serious thought. Alone in his bedroom, staring at the cracks in the ceiling, he replayed signing the contract. What had he done? The agreement had been signed with no idea of what would follow – without any inkling of Corelle's return. Now she was back…

He gulped back tears. Now his lover was back, he wanted to live – needed to live. Suicide was something for a man with no hope. His hope was alive in the beautiful smile that greeted him in the mornings, the bronze hue of the skin he caressed as she slept. The fact that she returned meant that he could curb his desire for underage girls. When he was with her, around her, he had no need for their bodies or minds. He was devoted to Corelle, who had left partly as a test to see if he could really change for good. He had slipped – he knew that – but *she didn't know*; and he saw no reason that she should. He had to get the contract annulled, and then he'd be free…

He leapt from his bed, frantically bounding across the room to the wardrobe, searching through the pockets of jeans and jackets like a man possessed. He retrieved the pink card, kissing it like a lost child. Wasting no more time, he picked up the phone and dialled the Suicide Note number, holding his breath while he waited for the connection.

There was nothing, then the dull *brrr* of a disconnected landline. Welling looked down at the handset in shock; he'd dialled a wrong number. He tried again, with the same result. Then again, hearing that *brrrr* once more. Panic gripped his gut. He slammed down the phone, his heart galloping in his chest, every sound and colour in the room vividly real and alive.

'*They finish the job within two weeks.*'

Grantham's calm voice reinforced his terror. He jumped to his feet, dressed without washing and left the flat, heading back to Shepherd's Bush.

He couldn't believe it. After buzzing the bell at the building entrance for near to ten minutes, he eventually got inside when someone came out and held the door open. He'd fairly run through the corridors until he found room D-474, with that blank unvarnished wood he remembered so well. Knocking tentatively provoked no response – louder knocks had no greater effect. Welling's panic increased until he was eventually pounding the door as hard as he could, screaming for someone to answer. Locks clicked and turned. He stepped back, taking huge gulps of breath and feeling relieved until he realised he'd been joined by someone from the next office.

'Can I help?'

It was a thirty-something white man – black loafers, 501s, Ben Sherman shirt tucked in at the waist – who was looking at his sweaty features, eyebrows arched in that eternal question he knew so well – *What the hell are you doing here?* Welling stared back at him, his panic forcing him not to react to the man's assumption that he must be up to no good.

'I'm looking for…' Realising how little he wanted to expose of his business took the words from his lips. '… the company that used to be based here. I have some unfinished business with them.'

'You and the rest of London,' the man returned. 'You're about the tenth person to come knocking on that door today. I don't know what's going on, and we never had much dealings with those guys, but they moved out almost a week ago.'

'Didn't they leave any forwarding address?' Welling tried not to sound desperate.

The man gazed at him, curious.

'No they didn't. We didn't even realise they'd gone until people started turning up,' he said, looking him up and down as he began to back away. 'Can I pass on a message?'

Welling shook his head before he turned and ran back down the corridor. The man watched him flee until he disappeared down the emergency stairs.

'Crazy people,' he muttered, then went into his office and forgot he'd ever met Paul Welling.

Every car, every person, every face was out to get him. He stumbled along the pavement, jumping at the sound of loud voices and car horns. On the tube, he leant against the sliding doors, furtive eyes moving from left to right, scanning the other commuters with an almost psychopathic gaze. People moved away until he was alone at his end of the carriage. Desolate, he slid whimpering to the floor, his arms clasped around his head, oblivious to the stares. When the amplified woman's voice informed him that he'd reached his station, he ran off the train, up the escalator, and jogged a complex route to his estate, full of twists and turns, so as to confuse anyone who might follow. He entered the tower block from the fire exit at the back of the building, taking the stairs until a woman came down with her laundry, scaring the shit out of him. He took the first empty lift he could find, arriving at his front door drenched in cold sweat. He locked the door behind him, then ran around the flat bolting the windows and patio door that led to his balcony.

When he got to the bedroom Corelle was already there, painting a potted Asiatic Lily that had just begun to bloom. He stopped in his tracks, unable to hide the beads of perspiration coursing down his head and body, saturating his thin T-shirt. She smiled in greeting, then frowned into the silence broken only by the harsh sounds of his breath. Her smile faded, replaced by a look of concern. She got to her feet, paintbrush in hand.

'What's up?'

Welling had to think fast – he couldn't let her know what was happening. She'd leave him for sure if she did.

'Nothing… I think I'm comin' down with flu or somethin' – I feel so weak…'

He staggered to the bed, lying down and closing his eyes, while Corelle sat down and watched him. The cool hand she laid on his forehead was a welcome respite from the heat that threatened to set his brain alight and combust his body. She felt both sides of his neck with the same careful attention that had been part of her

28

former job at the hospital. He opened his eyes and nearly cried when he saw the pity in hers.

'You've got a real bad temperature, Paul. It really does feel like flu. Come on, get those clothes off, you're going straight to bed.'

He complied, stripping to his boxers. She wrapped him up and disappeared into the kitchen, saying she was going to boil the kettle for some Beecham's Flu remedy. While she was gone, Welling quickly checked the window locks, making sure they were closed tight before jumping back into bed. Unable to stop himself, he began to shake in fear once more, teeth chattering, fingers clutching the duvet.

Corelle came back with a steaming mug, stopping dead when she saw the discomfort he was in. He tried desperately to stop his shaking limbs from jerking, but only made things worse. Corelle came closer, her pretty hazel eyes narrowed into thin slits of disquiet.

'Wow Paulie – you really *are* sick aren't you?'

He couldn't reply to such a precise statement. She sat on the edge of the bed, made him sit up and handed him the mug of Beecham's.

'It might be a bit hot, but I put some cold water in. Make sure you drink it down in one go.'

He nodded, playing along with the charade by taking the mug and knocking the warm mixture back, stopping for breath before finishing the rest. When he was done he thumped the mug onto the bedside cabinet, falling back onto the bed, wiping his lips and wincing at the taste. Corelle stroked his head, looking down on him. He blinked at her, feeling a mite better. At least he had Corelle in his life. A lot of men never even had that much.

'OK?' she asked. He nodded, silent, and she smiled once again. 'I love you to death, you big baby,' she continued, leaning over him to kiss his clammy head. He twitched, but she stroked his temple until he calmed down, her soothing touch as light as a cool breeze.

'Now sleep,' she ordered, still massaging.

He nodded in return and closed his eyes.

A deep, painful sting in his arm awakened him, intense enough to make him cry out. He tried to open his gummy eyes, but they were stuck together as if bonded with Super Glue. When he managed, the first thing he noticed was the darkness of the room – it took a moment more to realise that the curtains were closed and the lights were off. He felt drained of energy and strangely formless. He realised why a second later, when he tried to sit up. He couldn't move, couldn't feel his arms or legs. Both were completely numb.

He was paralysed.

'*Fuh… Fuh…*'

He was trying to scream the word *fuck*; but he couldn't even do that. His mouth was hanging open, and he had no control over its movements. He tried to turn his head. Nothing. He put all of his energy into what had been simple hours ago, straining the tendons and using all the will he possessed. Once again, nothing happened at first – but slowly, he got some power, and his head began to twist to the right. It was the hardest thing he'd ever done in his life, but he managed to turn enough to see his right arm.

When he focused on what he was doing, the fear returned in a flood that threatened to drown him alive where he lay.

An hand gripped his wrist. Another covered his fingers, which were wrapped around a pen, scrawling something onto the bottom of an A4 sheet of paper. He squinted, saw the sheet was ocean-blue – like the eyes of someone he'd once met – and another sheet of A4 he'd once seen. Focusing harder, he saw that the scrawl was his signature.

P. H. Welli

He took in the curves of an 'n' and a 'g' being formed, then his hand was released, to fall back onto the mattress with a thump. With great effort, he turned his head straight to find that he was sitting up, the duvet cover around his knees. Corelle moved from behind him, placing his back against the headboard, and walked in front of the bed. Her pretty features were set like concrete, the ocean-blue contract clutched in her hand like the pelt of a dangerous beast. In her other hand, she held a large hypodermic syringe, its barrel fully emptied of its contents. She held both up in front his eyes so he could see them. All trace of pity had left her eyes.

'Just a formality,' she said in a crisp tone devoid of emotion. 'We needed your last signature as conformation that I finished the job, as intended.'

Welling opened his mouth to scream, but the injection she'd given him had done its work. His body shuddered in spasms until his spirit fled.

DOUBLE ROOM

Friday

She knew he'd be trouble the moment she laid eyes on him. Not in a general sense, but for her. She knew he'd be trouble for her. He sported the type of look she found instantly attractive. Thick blond hair, curling at the front like the crest of a wave. Thin-yet-sharp eyes, blue as the sea that followed. Long thin nose, tanned skin, huge shoulders and to top it off he was tall; he had to be at least six-three. She watched him enter the lobby with the sour-faced woman by his side, head swivelling from left to right to take in the grandeur. From then on, it was impossible to quiet the sensation. Lust. A familiar feeling. She knew this man would cause her to do something bad.

Serena watched the couple approach the reception desk, smiling in her perfunctory way as the sour-faced woman took the lead. The woman was a head shorter than the man, and older – a great deal older. Dark pouches lurked beneath her eyes. Skin wrinkled and puckered like old fruit. There was no doubt about it; the woman had the face of a bitch. While her thoughts might be a little uncharitable, she knew she was as right about the woman as she was the man. Some people had faces shaped by their personalities. Faces that couldn't hide what they truly were. She'd worked the reception desk at Hoskins for almost two years. Serena was adept at watching people.

'Reservation for one double room please.'

'Certainly, Madam. Under what name?'

'Rivington. Stephanie Rivington.'

'Just checking reservations for you...'

The woman was as haughty as she expected. When Sour-Faced-Stephanie gave her name, she had even looked her square in the eyes as if she ought to have known who she was. Serena hadn't reacted. They were trained not to and she was good at her job. She simply let her eyes fall on her computer, her fingers onto the keys, tapping the name into the space provided.

'Here it is, Madam. I just need to take a swipe of your credit card.'

The woman nodded and dug around in her handbag. While her attention was diverted, Serena shot a glance at the attractive guy. He was strolling around the huge lobby with childlike wonder, admiring the crystal chandelier, running his hand along a marble vase and sniffing the bouquet within, inspecting the ancient elevator doors like a repair man. He must have sensed Serena's stare, for he turned as if tapped on the shoulder by an invisible finger. Before she knew what had happened they were looking into each other's eyes. The man smiled. The left corner of her lip gave a limp twitch, but she couldn't respond because at that moment the woman handed over the card with an amused expression, as if reading her thoughts. A faint blush lit Serena's cheeks as she took it, checked the signature, found the room key and handed it over. The woman was watching her like a scientist would a lab rat.

'Room 416. Take the lift to the top floor and follow the signs.'

'Thank you.'

The woman walked away from the desk. The attractive guy was still wandering around the lobby and that's when it happened, the thing that made her realise everything wasn't as cut and dried as she might have supposed. As the man inspected green glazed wall tiles with a curious finger, Stephanie came up behind him, grabbed his arm and tugged hard enough to make him stumble. Serena barely held back her gasp.

'Come on, stop playing around will you? I'm too tired for your rubbish tonight.'

The woman called the lift, which had been waiting on the ground floor. The doors parted. They stepped inside. She was turned sideways on, fixing the jacket of his suit and wiping invisible dust away, while the attractive man… did nothing. Stood inside the lift like an android whose power had failed, eyes blank, that same smile on his face, this time directed at the empty space before him. At no one. The woman finished her fussing and turned Serena's way just in time to catch her horrified gaze. And she grinned. A big, self-satisfied, *got-you-there* grin. She knew Serena had been so attracted she hadn't seen the truth. Before anything else could happen, the doors closed.

'Oh my God…'

One of the porters was pushing a set of suitcases across the lobby, close enough to hear. He looked up.

'Whassat, gorgeous?'

'Nothing… Nothing.'

Serena returned her gaze to the monitor, outrage burning her face.

Later that night she saw them heading for the restaurant. Serena was so popular at Hoskins she took liberties where other staff wouldn't dare (besides, it had long been rumoured that Richard the Duty Manager fancied her – they had fucked in the laundry room, but only twice and that was ages ago). She told a colleague she had an errand to run, and on the pretext of idle chat with the chefs and waiters, found that she could spy on the couple without arousing suspicion.

The woman was cutting the attractive man's food into minuscule pieces. Serving him impatiently, shovelling forkfuls into his mouth. Wiping surplus away from his chin like a mother does a toddler while the attractive man stared, blank, into the faces of other diners.

And she was rude. While her actions ought to have promoted love and good care, she performed them with disdain. When he didn't eat as fast as she liked, she pinched his arm and cajoled him. When he dribbled, she slapped his thigh hard enough to make him wince. Serena watched fellow diners get up and leave in silent protest, often staring at the couple in anger. One of the guys behind the bar made a move to go over and say something, but his manager grabbed him by the arm and shook his head. The barman stepped back, jaw rigid with anger.

Serena couldn't take much more after that. She went back to her desk wondering what the woman was out to prove.

It was unusually quiet for a Friday night, so there was time to look for the woman's name in the signing-in book and trace her finger across columns until she found the one marked *Company*. She memorised the name, got onto the internet, Googled and waited to see what came up. There were a few more check-ins after that, so it took a while before she could return to the list and find what she wanted. She double-clicked and the woman's company website emerged.

There was lots of information about different textiles and how long the company had been running, but that wasn't what Serena was looking for. Clicking on a link marked *CEO*, she was rewarded with a picture and some vague biographical information. Disappointed, she went back to her search engine and tried again, this time typing Stephanie Rivington's name. Up came a host of articles featuring the woman in pages from the *Financial Times* to *Marie Claire*. Serena trusted good old *Marie* to cover the angle she was looking for.

She was correct. The article began with the sentence: '...*Attractive CEO of Bard Textiles, Stephanie Rivington, has a lot to be proud of right now. This thirty-something powerhouse is ambitious, single...*'

And that *single* was all she needed to know. But why would she want to spend the weekend with someone like him? Didn't she care what anyone thought?

Then again, how bloody obvious was he really? Had fooled her enough to fancy him, and she was not nearly as old as Miss R...

Yeah. When she wasn't deriding him, when he was alone, he was something to behold. She saw it in the smiles of the bellboys (those that were that way inclined at least) and some of the female kitchen staff as they stood by the buffet tables. There was no doubt about it; the guy was sexy as hell. Enough for her to be his nursemaid in exchange for a weekend of fun? No. Serena didn't think so. But for a Plain Jane bordering forty with no romantic ties and a business doing so well she didn't have time for a partner... For a good fuck, then back to the office as if nothing had happened... Serena saw it all the time. Admittedly, it was usually men with young secretaries or working girls in tow, but sometimes there *were* women... though none as strange or cold as this one. Thinking about what she's seen made Serena's skin crawl. The half-formed idea, the one she'd had while looking into his eyes at the reception desk, cemented into a decision.

She would have him, Serena told herself, feeling her own little imp begin to dance. She would have him and nobody would know it but her...

Saturday

She entered Hoskins early that evening to begin her new shift. For most of the day her thoughts had circled around how she'd do it, glad her daughter was at her parents' so she had time to think. She strode into the lobby, smiling and accepting the usual compliments about how well she looked, then settled down behind the desk and immediately had guests to check in. Saturdays were always the busiest night by far, so there wasn't much time for staff small talk or skiving off; it was straight down to work. The steady flow of check-ins, room service orders and complaints about faulty showers and the like kept her too busy to pursue her plan. Close to midnight, everything slowed to normal speed. She looked up the room number on the computer. Room 416. Top floor. Begging a break from Richard, she decided to have a snoop around.

Hoskins was a truly massive building. The four star hotel had once been the headquarters of a national insurance firm housing five hundred offices, six main conference rooms and employing almost two thousand people. In the late seventies when the insurance company filed for bankruptcy, Hoskins took over the building and transformed the offices into bedrooms, the ballroom into a dining area, while retaining much of the original décor. Even now it was almost impossible to walk into the building for the first time without feeling a sense of awe.

First-timers often got lost in the labyrinthine corridors. When she first started at Hoskins the building sometimes even scared Serena. Two years there had developed her navigation; she knew every corridor, every short cut, every turn. Moving through back staircases and service lifts, she reached the top floor. 416 was at the far end of the corridor. She would knock and ask if everything was up to their requirements, if they needed anything. They would say no. Then she would leave. She knew the curiosity was meaningless, but she wanted to see him again. She was used to getting what she wanted.

Serena moved along the corridor, almost in a trance, her eyes fixed on the door. So it was a shock when a body suddenly slammed into hers, knocking her into the opposite wall, making her gasp as her right shoulder connected. She sagged when pain shot through her, collapsing onto the carpet with a cry. Her vision swam in front of her eyes, went dark. Serena took a deep breath, trying to calm herself. She became aware that the other person was moaning like a child.

Even before she raised her head, she knew who it was.

He was huddled against the far wall, crooning in a low voice, face pressed into the green tiles, body shaking. The suit he'd been wearing was gone, replaced by an un-ironed T-shirt and faded blue jeans. He looked more like a student than a grown man. She got to her feet, turning around to see if anyone was coming. No one was there.

Rubbing her bruised shoulder, she said, 'It's OK. Look, don't worry about me, I'm fine. Hey! Hey, look at me! Look, I'm OK; there's no need to panic, you didn't hurt me. I'm just a bit bruised that's all… Hey!'

Gently as she could, she grasped his chin with delicate fingers and turned his face around until he could see that she was all right. She smiled and felt a return of her lust as he looked at her through big blue eyes that seemed deep enough to dive into. She couldn't help herself, tracing a finger across his chiselled cheekbones to the cleft chin; he took in her own features, confused. They stared at each other, two shades of beauty face to face. His whimpers receded into nothing, his mouth working in rapid fits and starts.

'Soh… Soh… Sorry…'

'It's OK. I said it was OK, didn't I?'

She snatched another cautious look up and down the corridor before taking the plunge, nerves dancing. Grabbing the back of his head and leaning forwards she planted a kiss on his lips, holding it a minute before opening her mouth just a little and pulling away. She smiled.

'It's OK. Truthfully it is.'

When he didn't react, she frowned and looked a little harder, trying to find even the slightest form of expression; but there was nothing. She was just about to let him go and give up the chase, when he leant forwards by his own power and returned the favour, then looked into her eyes, just like she had his. It was her strangest, most innocent kiss ever.

'We should get out of here,' she said, almost to herself as much as to her new friend, aware that this was her opportunity. 'OK?'

No answer, just that lifeless stare. Even though the man had the ability to talk and communicate, it seemed he didn't use it much. Which was fine with her. All the men she'd been with in the past talked too much anyway.

'So what you doing out of your room at this time of night?'

The storeroom was a little musty, but warm. Only three people in the building had the key. She wasn't meant to be one of them, but she'd nicked Richard's and had a spare cut ages ago.

'Not gonna talk? Well you could at least tell me your name then. It's weird being intimate without knowing each other's names.'

She shrugged off her purple Hoskins jacket and placed it on a box of spare menus, followed by her blouse. It was very important that there were no stains.

'Have it your way then. I suppose it wouldn't be the first time for me. The not talking takes some getting used to though.'

He was standing with his back against the shelves, a hand unconsciously by his crotch – not moving, just poised as though in wait. She knelt down in front of him, unbuckled his belt, pulled down the jeans and boxers, then took him in hand. She stopped, looked up at him. His head was arched back so far all she could see was the lumpy bouncing ball of his Adam's apple. Serena frowned as she tugged.

'Do you talk to *her*? You must do innit, you must say something or the other. Why are you with her anyway? I'm talking about Stephanie. Honestly, she's twice your age, not even very attractive and she treats you like shite. You shouldn't let her do it you know.'

He was hard.

'*Very* impressive!'

She giggled. God, she was bad, but she loved every minute of it. She kept talking, even though he was breathing deeply and probably couldn't hear a word she was saying by now. In between sentences she took token licks, warming him up.

'A gorgeous guy like you… Shouldn't have to take that kind of abuse… You… should… be… stronger than that… Next time… She's mean to you… You should be mean to her… She deserves it…'

She had to speed things up. They'd been lucky so far, but if she wasted any more time they might be caught and she'd be sacked and she had a daughter to feed, so she couldn't have that. Serena took him halfway in, moving her fist along with her head, massaging his balls with her left hand while she did it. She was an expert, or so she'd been told. It wouldn't take long. Two minutes later he was moaning in a voice louder than any she'd heard from him so far. Her mouth grew sticky and warm. She got to her feet, searched in her jacket pockets. All she had was some scrap paper, so she used that to spit into, folding it carefully, making sure nothing spilt. They had to leave no traces, particularly as she planned to corner Richard again some time in the near future. He wouldn't be pleased if he found out what she'd done.

'You OK?'

The man was panting and looking at her like a puppy gazing at its mother. She pulled up his jeans and buckled his belt, kissed him on the lips, then gave him a hug for good measure. He didn't hug her back, but she didn't mind. She'd had him. Not in the way she'd really wanted, but probably the only way that was possible. She guessed he wasn't very good at the penetration bit anyway, the way he was and all. And truth be told, Serena was already losing interest. She just wanted to get him out of the storeroom, back to where he belonged.

Stephanie. Serena smiled at the thought of the CEO.

'So you remember what I said? OK?' Her voice was kindly as she led him out of the room, checked to make sure everything was as it was, then locked the door and took him down the corridor. 'You don't have to take her shit. If someone hits you, hit them back, that's what me mam always taught me and I think she was right. Don't stand for it, you're a big hardback man. All right?'

He was staring at her, blank as a whitewashed wall. She sighed and led him up the staff stairs to his floor.

'Go on. Go to your room.'

He stood there, a smile on his face. He reached for her hand.

'No!' Despite her fear, she couldn't help a coy grin. 'Stop it you... Go on, go back to Stephanie. She'll be missing you by now.'

He reached again. This time she slapped his hand away.

'*No!*' She pointed down the corridor. 'Back. Go... Back.'

He looked at the floor, down-mouthed. She felt more than a little exasperated. He wasn't worth losing her job over. He had to go. She was wondering how to get the message across when he suddenly began to walk away quickly, without looking back, taking long strides.

'See you tomorrow!'

He didn't turn. She closed her eyes. When she opened them, he was gone.

Richard went mad when she got back. She'd said ten minutes and she'd taken half an hour. She promised she'd add it to the end of her shift. That kept him sweet enough to pinch her arse when no one else was around and she let him do it, glad he was still showing an interest. They'd been quite friendly at one point, 'mates that fuck' as she'd put it, before he started seeing some white girl from Rusholme and seemed to lose his appetite. Apparently the white girl wasn't enough of a serving now as he'd been sniffing around her again for the last week. Serena had decided to keep him on a loose leash and only reel him in when he was needed. She knew what game he was playing. Even though she was up for taking part, she smarted at the knowledge that he would never make her his girlfriend, even though she didn't want him either.

Her friends wondered why she constantly dated white men. She was drop dead gorgeous, had a great body and was a right laugh too. They weren't being racist (so they said), but didn't she ever, for once in her life, want a shapely arse, full lips, dark skin, in bed beside her? She had a Black daughter so she had to know what that felt like. Didn't she ever miss the feel of a Black man?

Though she told no one this, Serena often pondered that question. Yes, she did like Black men – Denzel, Wesley, Tyrese, D'Angelo, Maxwell. The trouble was, there weren't many decent ones in the flesh. Most of the ones she'd met she wouldn't touch with anyone's bargepole and she couldn't say why, just that she never seemed to click with them in the way that she did with... others. And it wasn't that she was ashamed to be Black. If anyone thought that, they couldn't be more wrong. Her dad had made sure she knew her history, both the Caribbean and African stuff and not just slavery either. But she was half and half. Her friends had to accept that. They saw her as Black, but half of her wasn't and there was nothing she could do to change that. Nothing she *would*. Still, she couldn't help wondering why she hadn't been with a Black guy since her ex. Why white guys – even retarded white guys for fuck's sake – seemed like so much of a better deal.

Though it had only just happened, she was beginning to feel guilty. She wasn't used to it. Though she tried not to think about what she'd done, the longer her shift went on, the more impossible it became. The man was mentally disabled. She'd known that. She'd taken advantage. What did that say about her?

Serena was so deep in thought that the remainder of her shift went by before she knew it, even the extra half-hour. She usually larked about with Richard before she left. Today she got her coat and sneaked from the building without a word to anyone.

Sunday

It was two a.m.. Serena sat by her reception desk reading Toni Morrison's *The Bluest Eye*, which she'd started years ago and never quite managed to finish. She knew full well why she'd picked the book from her shelf, but she was finding it difficult to maintain enthusiasm. No doubt, part of the reason was the concentration needed to read at work – which was hard to find, despite the quiet of the approaching dawn. The rest was down to Stephanie's companion. What she had done to him.

She'd checked the computer when she arrived that evening. They were still there. There was really no reason to be worried about the guy letting the cat out of the bag or behaving strangely, but… Breakfast, lunch and dinner had been delivered via room service. They hadn't been seen together since the previous day.

The reception buzzer went off, loud in the quiet of the huge lobby, making Serena jump. She placed a hand on her breast to steady her heart, laughed and automatically reached for the phone, then caught sight of a light flashing in front of her. Her hand froze as though infected with sudden rigor mortis.

It was 416. Their room. It was their room and she had to answer.

She picked up the receiver as if it were a poisonous snake. *You knew he'd be trouble*, her mind was cursing, *you knew and you still went and did it…*

'Good morning, reception…'

Say it just the way she was meant to, raising her pitch at the end just like they were any old customers…

'Soh… Soh… Sorry…'

'I beg your pardon?'

She looked around the lobby to see who might overhear. Richard had disappeared ages ago and was probably sleeping in a spare room. The two graveyard shift porters were in the staff room playing gin rummy and the cooks weren't due for another three hours. She was on her own.

'Sorry…'

The phone disconnected before she could say his name. *Shit*. She didn't evenknow his name. And what was all that about anyway, calling reception saying one word then putting the phone down? It was a cheek, a waste of her fuckin' time. She wished he'd learn something else to say for God's sake. Sorry was the only word she'd ever heard him speak and that was only when he'd…

'Oh no…' she covered her mouth with a hand. 'Oh Jesus no…'

She stood up, made sure her key card was attached to her waist. Walked to the lift and pressed the call button. Stepped in and took Otis to the fourth floor. Walked along the bare corridor until she was standing outside room 416.

All was quiet. In her ears there was a roar that was her own voice, her own voice saying –

'A gorgeous guy like you shouldn't have to take that kind of abuse... Next time she's mean to you... You should be mean to her... She deserves it...'

And he was big wasn't he? Big enough to hurt near enough anyone, especially a small middle-aged woman. The guy was a retard, which meant he was open to suggestion wasn't he? Look how easy it had been to lead him to the storeroom.

And she had goaded him into hurting the woman.

She knocked on the door, timid at first, with more strength when she heard nothing. She pressed her ear to the wood, straining for a voice...

'Hello... Hello...'

It was the woman and she sounded in pain. Serena had been right. Something had happened.

She slipped in her key card, and went inside. There was a shadowy darkness in the room and she couldn't see very much. The TV was on, showing a late night cable flick. She could hear the shower, though it sounded as if the water was hitting tiles, not a human body. She went to turn it off. It was giving her the creeps. Her eyes adjusted to the dark.

That was when she saw Stephanie Rivington.

She was handcuffed to the bedposts by both hands. All Serena could see of her face was eyes. Her mouth must have moved, because there was that strange croak.

'... You... Reception Girl...'

'Yes Ms. Rivington, it's me,' she said in her best hotel voice. 'Now do you know where the keys to the cuffs are so that I can release you? Then I'll go back to my desk and we won't say any more about this, will we?'

'... It was him... He did this...'

Serena rummaged in the bedside cabinet, wanting to leave. He obviously wasn't around but she didn't know how long that would last and she definitely didn't want him to think she'd get involved in this freaky sex scene. She wasn't into bondage.

'Now Ms. Rivington, you know that's none of my business. If you'll just tell me where the keys are...'

The light. She needed more light. Serena moved to the main switch and made to touch it.

'You fucked him… Didn't you?'

She stopped dead.

'Last night… Sent him to the machine to get some cigarettes… Didn't get back for ages… Saw the way you were looking at him…'

She couldn't face her. Not and tell the truth; no way.

'Ms. Rivington–'

'Turn on the light!' The woman began to scream. 'Look at what he did to me!'

She almost left right there and then. Walked out of the door, down the corridor and through the Hoskins lobby never to return. Because she didn't want to know, not really. She forced herself to press the switch and turn to face Stephanie Rivington. The CEO was naked and covered with blood from head to toe. It saturated the blankets; she couldn't understand why she hadn't smelt it before. It trailed down her forehead like thick red perspiration, running along the slight curve of her breasts and stomach, pooling in the crevice of her crotch like a muddy puddle of rain. The sheets were a deep dark red that looked slick and wet as fresh paint. And while she stared at this woman who looked more like a horror movie victim than a human being, her selfishness and conscience joined hands and hid. Then all that was left was the shock of what she was seeing, the quiet violence of what had been done.

'See…' Stephanie whispered.

The door clicked. Heart in mouth, Serena turned around. Someone was coming. Stephanie pointed at the door and began screaming as loudly as her dry throat would allow. Serena moved away from the door, wanting to bawl in fear.

'It's him, he's coming, it's him –'

'Shut up!' she found herself snapping before flooding with instant regret. 'Wait a minute, let me think…'

There was no time for thought. The door opened and there he was, standing in the doorway looking at her with a maniac's gleam in his eye. He frowned at the sight of her, stepping further into the room. His creased T-shirt was spotted with Stephanie's blood. When he raised his left hand she could see the glint of the razor blade and wondered how he'd walked the corridors without being seen, before she remembered the time of morning. Still, she wished that Richard or somebody else had faced the guy down before he'd come back to this room. A voice burrowed its way through the roar in her ears.

'Get him, get him, get him quick –'

'Soh… Sorry…' the attractive guy was saying.

Stephanie's fear prompted her own. As he lumbered closer Serena grabbed the nearest thing she could find, a huge vase, and threw it as hard as she could. He ducked and stumbled. Serena bolted through the open door, ignoring Stephanie's curses and ran, ran as hard as she could. She didn't dare wait for the lift, leaping the stairs, almost breaking her ankle, down four flights that seemed to go on forever, finally running into the lobby in a jumble of hair, eyes and Hoskins clothing. Richard was behind her desk by then, looking ready to let rip until he saw the tears flowing down her cheeks. She ran at him full pelt, hugging him hard and letting the dam burst, hearing the frown in his voice as he asked her what was wrong.

When she calmed down, Serena told him.

The ambulance came, police came. They even called the fire department when it became apparent that the key to the handcuffs was lost. Sitting at the reception desk with a blanket around her shoulders, Serena watched him being led towards a TSG by two large police officers. Thought, *He still looks sexy*, then wondered how she could allow that thought. Hadn't she learnt, yet? The guy's head was bowed, his expression a mask of sorrow. He averted his eyes from the desk as though he'd been told not to look. Serena sipped at her coffee and watched him walk out of her life.

Ten minutes later a bandaged Stephanie appeared, wheeled out of the lift by paramedics and towards the lobby doors. The CEO waved a mummified hand in her direction. Serena shrugged off her blanket, put down the coffee and followed. She flashed her sweetest smile at the paramedics, both male, and asked if she could have a quick word in private. They grumbled a bit, then agreed to let them speak for just a minute. Thanking them, she knelt in front of the wheelchair.

'Hi there…'

'Hello.'

Stephanie's croaking voice was gone, though her vocal chords still seemed strained and husky.

'What are we like then, eh?'

'Like high school girls I reckon.'

You more than me, Serena thought, but she wasn't arguing.

'So... They give you any painkillers?'

'An injection,' Stephanie whispered. 'It's doing the trick.'

They smiled at each other. Serena touched her shoulder.

'I'm really sorry this happened to you, Miss Rivington. Truth-fully, I am.'

'Don't you worry. Serves me right for not picking someone nearer my own age.'

She gave a woozy smile and closed her eyes. Close up, Serena could see her cuts for the first time. None on her face or neck, but several straight slashes taped with white plasters just above her hairline. Strange. The rest were presumably beneath the band-ages wrapping her arms and legs. Serena leant as close as she dared.

'Look... I just had to tell you... I'm sorry about my role in all this mess, I really am. And... Look, I'm grateful that you didn't tell anyone what I did. With him... I need this job, so... Thank you, Miss Rivington.'

The women appraised each other once more.

'A favour for a favour,' Stephanie replied, bursting into a sudden smile, her voice a husky singsong. 'I won't tell if you won't tell...'

That didn't sound right. What was she going on about? It was the drugs, Serena concluded.

'What d'you mean?'

Nothing for a moment, then Stephanie grabbed Serena's hand and squeezed, even though it seemed to cause her pain.

'Allan's such a dependable boy... Open to any suggestions, as you well know, Ms. Reception Girl... It's amazing the things I got him to do this weekend... He'd never held a razor blade before, can you believe it? Wasn't allowed to I suppose... Ah well... He'll have to learn to think for himself now, where he's going. After all, anyone could take advantage... Couldn't they?'

Serena snatched her hand away, looking down at Stephanie in disbelief. The CEO put a finger to her lips and smiled again.

'Goodbye, Ms. Reception Girl…'

The paramedics were back, wheeling her onto the ramp and into the ambulance. Some twenty minutes later Serena was standing at the same spot, rigid, as the north wind chilled her tears.

GOLD

He used to be handsome. In the old days of school and children's television, run-outs and penny sweets, he had been the apple of many an eye. As a youth he'd been a 'sweet boy', charming the girls, and even some women, with a natural ease. There had been many moments, each one creating a tiny smile that tugged at the corners of his lips, even now. When the memory was strong, recollections of young flesh rubbing against young flesh made him squirm against the hard concrete, shake his head to dispel the desperate, overwhelming thoughts, grab Styler tight and hug her to him just to have contact with something, anything that was alive. It had been a long time between then and now. It pained him to think he was the only one who realised how much of a transformation had taken place.

It was the final week before Christmas. Those dark days of tense shoppers, eager children and downhearted adults, grim at the prospect of a 'merry' holiday. Maybe they'd feel more like celebrating if snow fell this year; but this was London and there hadn't been a White Christmas for over twenty years. Even today, sitting on the corner where All Saint's meets Westbourne Park Road, red blanket spread beneath him as though for a picnic, Laramie found himself covered in a light spray of rain that had been falling since early dawn. He looked down at Styler, curled up against his thigh as tightly as she could manage, black fur flecked with what resembled a million tiny diamonds. Laramie could lose himself in such detail, sink into the hypnotic patterns to be found on Styler's fat torso, just to escape embarrassed denials of his existence from those who passed his corner.

He looked up, just in time to see her walking along All Saint's towards him, shoes clicking, Fendi bag swinging, Burberry patterned umbrella held at an angle to avoid the lampposts, smiling as she reached his spot.

'Hi there!'

'You all right?'

'How are you dis mornin'?'

'Well… Not too bad today, thanks. You?'

'I'm OK… A bit late for work actually… Aren't you gettin' wet?'

Sometimes they, The Public, asked the most stupid questions, even her.

'Yeah, I am a bit actually…'

'You can borrow my umbrella,' she said, with that tone of finality he already knew she couldn't help. 'But I want it back, so look after it. I'll get it from you after work.'

He was too surprised to think of refusal. When he'd leant the massive umbrella at an angle that covered both himself and Styler, she smiled as though it was her in the dry. Producing a handful of gold coins, she let them fall into his already waiting palm with a series of dull clunks. Five. Laramie's gaze fell into his lap.

'God bless you.'

He made himself look her in the eye. She smiled down, cocoa butter cheeks deepening into a warm red she actively fought to contain, the struggle making her seem even more alluring. In the old days… In the old days he would have said one line and she would have been his. Now it was hard enough to say one coherent word without stuttering and making a fool of himself.

'Dat's all right. You stay strong, black man, OK? I'll see you at lunch.'

'Thanks…'

She was already crossing the street, leaving him a glimpse of a perfect smile and the steady, businesslike walk that had first caught his attention, rump swaying like a metronome. He watched as she entered the jewellers shop, mouth moving in a greeting too far away for him to hear, and then disappearing down into the basement. The five gold coins lay in his palm, warm from contact with hers. He put them away and prepared for lunch.

At precisely one p.m. she pushed open the jewellers shop door and re-crossed the street, making a beeline for him. The light rain had long stopped falling. Her umbrella lay beside him, designer wings folded like a pigeon awaiting flight. Styler caught a whiff of her scent and jumped up, letting out quick barks of greeting until he quieted her. She was holding a steaming black mug. As she got closer, Laramie could see the orange RIZLA logo slapped across one side. She was still wearing her enormous smile.

'Hello…'

'Hey.'

'Thought you might fancy a cup of tea?'

'Yes please.'

She gave him the mug, trying to avoid Styler's prying nose.

'Careful, it's hot.'

'Styler, get out of it! *Sit! Sit!* Good girl.'

The young woman crouched down beside him. It was difficult to look at her directly. Every feature she possessed was beautiful. Her hair was braided in intricate canerows that fell to the back of her neck and brushed against her collarbone. Her eyes were shaped like sesame-seeds; the pupils bottomless black pits that threatened to swallow him whole. Her cheeks were chubby and dimpled, the faint, almost-blush still apparent. Her lips were wheat-coloured, tiny on her face. Without the jacket, her cream linen blouse and skirt flowed over her curves; Laramie imagined he could hear the garments sigh in ecstasy each time she shifted on her heels.

'So, what's your name?'

He'd been so busy looking her over, a noticeable silence had fallen. Embarrassed, he turned his gaze to the grimy paving slabs.

'Laramie…'

'I'm Blaine. Pleased to meet you! What ends you from, Laramie?'

'East…'

'East! You're a long way from home ain' you? What brings you all the way to Grove den, if yuh don't mind me askin'?'

'Uh…'

Laramie began to stutter, now truly unable to remember what he'd been attempting to block since he first began treading London streets. It was so long ago, blurred by alcohol, trips and crack, by violent beatings from random strangers, jail cells and a thousand screaming faces all merging into one huge super-being. Greying hair, distressed eyes, pious expression... The face of his mother as he'd last seen her... Even though she never said a word of condemnation, Laramie could feel her displeasure wash over him like a cold shower.

'Me and... girlfriend... Had a fight... Rent was due... Had to work...'

A pounding pain began to surge through his forehead. He groaned aloud and clutched his temples. In an instant there were strong fingers at the base of his neck, kneading with a power that forced him to relax. Styler stirred to see what she was doing, cocked her head to one side and settled on the blanket when she realised nothing untoward was going on. Laramie couldn't help but close his eyes.

'Hey, hey, don't you work yourself up for nuffin'. You don't have to tell me if it bothers you... I understand. God, who ain' bin through shit these days, eh? I've had enough of my own to know that sometimes it's all best left behind you, innit Laramie?'

'Yeah...'

Blaine made him feel weak. He was powerless to stop her. Why else would he think of his mother today, when he'd managed for so long without feeling her presence? It was Blaine, he concluded. It had to be Blaine.

'I know how it is, man, you don't hafta tell me nuffin'. I've been through nuff shit in my short life-span, you know, stuff you probably wouldn't believe; but I've always had self-belief. I always thought that I could control my own destiny – does dat make any sense? I feel like, you know, I can be anyone I wanna 'cos it's all about havin' a positive mind state, don't you reckon? Right about now, you see me working in a jewellers an' dat, but dat ain' what I'm really about... What I'm really about is singin' man... I've done it all my life you know, on an' off, not professional or nuffin, more like singing in the shower, but everyone tells me I sound like Ashanti and I think I'm quite good, so I thought why not give it a go...'

On and on she went, a virtually ceaseless flow of chatter that drenched him in its torrent, requiring him only to nod his head and mutter one word replies at best. Not that he minded; it had been so long since anyone had spoken to him like a normal human being. Laramie found himself smiling at the sheer pleasure of close contact, nodding with false animation whenever someone walked by (*Look at me! I'm holding a normal conversation with a normal person, look how normal I am!*), trying but failing to follow her train of thought, which led from singing, to having to pay rent, to having to find a better job, to her current job, to her frustration with the lack of good-looking male staff in the jewellers, then finally onto her single status and how sick she was of men anyway, so sick, she'd probably die alone.

At that point, Blaine's relentless pace slowed and then came to a halt. She looked at her watch, heaved a massive breath of surprise, and got to her feet. Styler looked up, only this time she let her head sink back to the pavement, already accustomed to the young woman's presence.

'I better go an' get some lunch.' She gestured for the mug. He passed it over, shielding his eyes from the sun. 'I like talkin' to you. If it was up to me I'd have you in the shop, drinking tea and keeping me company, but the boss would go spare. Says I skive enough already!'

'Don't worry about it.'

'It's a shame though…' she beamed his way again. 'All right den, I'll see yuh tomorrow if you're here. Same time, same place!'

He forced himself to grin in return. After all she deserved *something*.

'I'll be here.'

Blaine's smile faded. She bent over and kissed his unshaven cheek, seemingly immune to the odour, scratched Styler's neck and was off without another word. This time, he couldn't bear to look.

The next day he was there early, laying his red rug down sometime before 8 am, across from the shop doors. The air was damp and warm, the greyness all-consuming. Styler seemed to have caught his mood; she too faced the thick steel door, with her chin resting against her paws, eyes closed tight as if to ward off the world. He stroked her and they shared a packet of shortbread biscuits. An old woman dropped fifty pence into his lap.

By 9:30 he knew something was wrong. Laramie was familiar with the routine – he'd been sitting at his corner long enough to know what time the staff came and went. Today, there was only one, a spotty white kid he'd never met, pacing around outside the closed doors, looking at his watch with obvious impatience. He waited ten minutes before trying his mobile. After another ten he turned left and walked quickly up Westbourne Park Road without looking back. Laramie didn't blame him – a day off was a day off. For a long time after, nothing happened.

Then Blaine came speed-walking down All-Saint's, a set of jangling keys in her hand, her expression fixed and serious. She hurriedly unlocked the shop doors and disappeared inside without a single glance in his direction. Laramie tried to disassociate himself from the hurt, the ache that made his stomach churn, but he couldn't deny he'd been looking forward to seeing her. But what could he expect? She was a jeweller's assistant; he was a guy on road. That was the basis of their friendship. He would do well to bear that in mind.

Nevertheless, it took until 11:30 for him to realise she wasn't coming out. He focused hard on the pavement, steeling his eyes.

Sometimes he sat on the red blanket looking at the speckled grey of paving slabs until his senses dulled and the noise of the outside world faded like the final notes of a ballad. No sound, no odour, no sensation or touch could penetrate the cocoon he created. Then he could dive so deep inside his head that there was nothing but darkness around him, thick like honey yet light as air. He could lose the feeling in his arms and legs, head and torso and become free to move in a way that felt real though dreamlike, something between swimming and flying. In the darkness, he had the certainty of a shark, the grace of a bird.

He could even travel to other places. Though the dark seemed never-ending and he had no sensation of actually moving, if he concentrated hard enough, there was a strong push of gravity and a breathless feeling in his chest, a snap and he was there – wherever he wished *there* to be – alive and real, the whole human being he remembered. Handsome, young, charming, able to do *anything*. Admired even by his enemies. He could live his life as the person he should have been.

He was just beginning another descent into the depths when he felt Styler move beside him. He opened his eyes. Blaine. She was dressed all in black today, black shirt, black trousers, black shoes. Her dress sense matched the stern look on her face.

'Hello, Laramie.'

'Hey. What's goin' on?'

'What d'you mean?'

The look was gone in an instant, replaced by the sheepishness of a teenager caught sneaking in to the house way past their curfew.

'The shop. You was late openin' today innit?'

She sighed. Another change of face. Now she looked pissed off. 'Oh, *dat*. Yeah, the boss's daughter is ill or somethin', so no one was around to open up. Little Miss Muggings over here was meant to have the morning off but Gavin's phone's switched off, so that leaves me on me own for the rest of the day. Fuckin' *marvellous*. Anyhow, it's kinda quiet, so there's no reason why you can't come in an' have dat cup of tea we was talkin' about.'

She seemed tall as a giant, looking down on him as if he was some alien creature she wanted to probe. He squinted.

'What about your boss?'

'He's not *here* is he? And I stopped the tape. No one'll know.'

'I dunno man…'

'Don't be a scaredy cat…' she giggled. 'C'mon, don't blow me out! You can keep me company. It'll be good.'

He looked up at her, open-mouthed.

'Come *on*…'

'OK… OK…'

He got to his feet and grabbed Styler's lead.

'Dunno about the dog though.'

'She's comin' or I'm stayin'.'

'All right, all right. Cor, anybody would think I'm askin' you to drink rat poison the way you're goin' on! I'm tryin' to be friendly!'

He staggered across the road with the girl, regretting his

decision already, joints stiff from sitting so long, head fuzzy from his dreams. Styler trotted along by his side, content.

'Not many friends... I got... Don't need 'em...'

She guided him through steel doors. At his feet, Styler was immediately alert, aware that this was a brand new place to explore, full of original smells and sights and curious items. She stood stiff as a board, nose twitching uncontrollably. Blaine was smiling again, now that she'd got her way.

'We all need friends,' she said in a tone that expected no argument. 'We can't exist without 'em.'

He chose to ignore her, waiting as she locked the door behind them, following her down long, steep steps that led to the basement. Wooden-framed display cases lined purple walls, each filled with all kinds of gold, sealed with a glass door and a huge silver lock that gleamed in the rectangular spotlights. Laramie peeked inside one of the cases and looked away when he saw the price tags. At the bottom of the steps was a small counter and office area: filing cabinet, desk lamp, jewellers' paraphernalia (penlight, magnifying glass, thin and strange-looking metal tools). Blaine slid her firm body around the desk, beckoning when she saw him lagging behind looking down-in-the-mouth.

'Oh come on man, don't look like that. I'm not gonna eat you! Take a seat here and I'll get dat kettle on, all right?'

'Yeah sure – Styler, *sit!*'

'Think she'd like some water?'

'Love some.'

'OK.'

She disappeared around a corner where he presumed the staff room was. Now they were inside, Styler was unusually subdued considering the attractions surrounding them. Laramie could not produce a matching disdain. Any ordinary member of The Public would feel the same, wouldn't they? Want to sniff around, touch the furnishings, admire the extravagant décor and appreciate the bargains to be had. Getting to his feet, he took deep breaths, telling himself he was good enough; he was only taking a look. Window shopping. He imagined himself as a minute speck of dust floating though one of his dream worlds. Able to go any-where and touch anything he pleased.

In a narrow strip of walkway created by a nearby wall and the alcove of the stairs, Laramie found a flat screen television mounted like a piece of modern art. The display advertised cut-price designer clothes. As he watched, Versace jeans, Polo shirts and Evisu jackets all came and went one after another. He came to another display case, larger than those on the walls, in the centre of the basement floor like a huge chest of drawers. The shop entrance was above. Laramie could see The Public going about their business through the huge windows. Some looked down into the glittering interior of the shop, though none appeared to notice him. He stepped closer to the display case. More rich people's toys. A 22 carat stopwatch, a solid looking bracelet, even a gold-plated set of tweezers. The items were all second hand. It dawned on Laramie that this seemingly elegant jewellers shop was in fact a pawnbrokers. He walked under the landing of the shop entrance. Here he found a glass cage containing a lizard sitting on a lump of wood amid lush leaves, motionless. It looked too still to be real, until it blinked twice. Laramie shook his head. Only in Ladbroke Grove.

'It's real yuh know.'

She was holding another mug of tea, looking pleased at his curiosity.

'I know. I saw it blink couple times.'

'It's an iguana. We feed it veggies and fruit every day. They used to make me do it and it really shit me up, but now I don't mind. I practically beg to do it nowadays.'

They were silent for a long time, watching the reptile do nothing.

'Don't seem right really. Locking up an animal like this in a cage for us to stare at,' he grumbled at last.

Even that seemed to please her, though she said nothing for a time, staring at him with only a hint of a smile, until he was once again forced to stare at the lizard, feeling her gaze creep up his face like a bug.

'Is that why you sleep on the street? 'Cos you wanna be free?'

He tried not to grimace. She'd love that explanation. At some point in her life, she'd probably even mulled over the idea of that type of freedom for herself... a movie star liberty, a Thelma and

56

Louise style runaway's dream that never worked out as planned. Laramie had seen plenty with that dream in their eyes – mostly kids from up North, though sometimes adults, all thinking they'd left their problems behind. Wherever you ran, you took yourself with you. The freedom of the open road was not his story.

'Somefing like dat...' he mumbled in response.

'I only say it 'cos dis iguana made me think ah you. It's almost like you're on display, sitting on that blanket outside on the corner, don't yuh reckon? For different reasons though, way different. I mean, they put dis iguana here for the customers really, to make dem come inside and buy the crap they sell. I reckon the government leaves you lot out there cos it reminds people what'll happen if you drop out, don't follow the rules, you know. Beware, don't end up like dem type ah ting. I reckon...'

She broke off as she caught a flash of hurt in his eyes. He turned away and walked towards Styler, who was watching them both from behind the counter. Before he could get there, Blaine was grasping his elbow, forcing him to stop. He snatched his arm away.

'Wha' you doin'?'

'I'm sorry. Sometimes I open my mouth an' shit comes out, I know it does. I never meant to offend you.'

Her eyes were so wide and sincere he wanted to cry. They were the eyes of a newborn baby, filled with hope and innocence, alertness and curiosity, naked to the world. She made a sad face and before he could stop her, she hugged him to her full breast as though he was her son. She was warm, oh so warm and soft, too soft to let go. Yes, he was embarrassed, but it had been so long since he had been handsome. It was a feeling he recognised, like laying eyes on a place he had once been to as a child. He was paralysed by her comfort, not resisting, not moving in case she got scared and let him go. But she held him, crooning into his ear as though providing him with a prayer all of his own, a prayer he could take out into the world and show like a passport to all those who didn't understand. She knew him, that's what it felt like. The feeling was so good Laramie wanted to melt away right there on the spot.

'It's okay, Black man, I know, I know... Dis some hard shit you're goin' through innit, dis life shit... Hard to believe I know, but we're all feelin' it from some degree to another… Have to do tings you might not want to in order to survive, innit though? I know, I bin there, man, more dan once. I read my Bible man, read dat good so don't worry, Larry, I won't shun you like the other people do. I'm always here fuh you, I want you to know dat right now, Laramie. I see what's behind all this,' she eased her grip on his body and the relative cold of the air shot through him. He wanted her back. As if reading his mind, she picked at his clothes quickly and grasped him close again. '… The dirt and the smell… I don't care about dat 'cos I see what you are… A strong Black man, ain' dat right, Larry? A strong Black man…'

She was gripping him so tight she couldn't see his face. He was glad of it. No one would see the raw grimace that appeared over her right shoulder as he closed his eyes. When he opened them, a group of tourists wearing heavy-looking puffa jackets were grouped outside the steel doors of the shop, peering inside like visitors to the zoo. One of them tried the door and a couple of the others cupped gloved hands to their faces, squinting. He watched them and tapped Blaine on the shoulder.

'Got company.'

Her face fell.

'Oh *no*. We never get anyone in here usually, not at this time. There aren't even any appointments…'

'So what d'you wanna do?'

He was stern, already preparing to leave.

'I gotta let 'em in, Larry. You wait in the back while I see what they want an' we'll take it from there, OK?'

'I don't wanna get you in trouble…'

'It's *OK*… You won't. Just go through there…'

He let himself be pushed in the direction of a door that said **NO ENTRY**. The tourists were still ringing the bell above him, while Blaine concentrated on getting him to move. There was a short corridor beyond this door, with a door to the right that led to the staff room, a small space where someone had tried to create a homely feeling with household items and prints of famous paintings. He stood in the centre of the room, not knowing where to put himself. Styler was circling at his heel, equally uncomfortable.

'Wait, I'll be back in a bit.'

She was gone before he could turn and face her. He looked around, bending over and pushing Styler's hindquarters until she sat, finding a chair and doing likewise. There was a dining table beside him bearing a collection of newspapers. Laramie hadn't read one for years. There were prints and posters everywhere; health and safety adverts, a pin-up board filled with glossy colour photos, some of which had a smiling Blaine as the central figure, each picture taken on the shop floor, male staff members posing with their arms around her waist, baring teeth like wolves before a kill. That was when he noticed the box sitting in solitary splendour on top of the fridge; small and rectangular, covered in blue felt with a thin gold trim around the lid. A jewellery box. He was intrigued and picked up the box, turning it over in his fingers for a moment. He prised open the lid to see five tiny gold rings, half-moon shapes, solid as miniature wedding rings. He stared, mesmerised, knowing what he wanted, looking up at a black and white Blaine jerkily showing the herd of tourists around the shop floor. Keeping his eyes on the monitor, he replaced the lid, allowing his hand to close around the jewellery box, push it through a hole in his left pocket and into the lining of his jacket as he used to years ago. He went back to the chair, still watching the monitor, unaware that his dog was studying him: slightly puzzled, head cocked to one side, full of admiration and respectful fear.

It took Blaine twenty minutes to show the tourists around the shop, open some of the cases, and eventually get them to buy a few small items. When Laramie saw them leave he got to his feet, checked that the box couldn't possibly be seen, and dragged Styler out of the staff room.

'Hey!'

Blaine was smiling, no doubt pleased with her efficient handling of a potentially tense situation. He couldn't look at her pretty face without feeling bad, even though it was a matter of survival. If he'd told her about the rings, or been with her when he'd seen the jewellery box, there was even the possibility that she might have given it to him anyway, wasn't there?

Laramie thought so.

'How'd it go?'

'They bought a set of cufflinks and a few other bits and pieces. They only wanted trinkets for some friends back in Germany.' Blaine's smile faded as she noticed his zipped up jacket and the urgent way he was tugging at Styler's lead. 'Wha' you doin'?'

'I gotta go. It's not right me being here. Besides, I need to feed her.' He nodded down at the dog panting by his feet.

'Don't be silly.' Blaine's smile returned, slow and hesitant this time. 'They've gone now. They didn't even see you.'

'Yeah, but there'll be others later. You can't expect me to spend all day in the staff room. I gotta go.'

He walked up the slanted steps with Blaine trailing behind, still attempting to talk him round. At the solid metal door he turned to face her.

'I appreciate everything you've done…'

'Wha' you talkin' about, Larry? I only give you a cup ah tea.'

A wave of melancholy swept through him. She'd trusted him and he'd betrayed her. He couldn't look her in the eye.

'I gotta go.'

He could feel her disappointment.

'See you then…'

Laramie only looked around when he reached his usual corner. She was gone, the shop doors firmly closed. He walked on past his spot, not wanting to be there when she left work in the evening, not knowing where his guilty steps would take him.

He avoided the corner for a long time afterwards, moving as far as Kensal Rise. He found a dusty room on a building site that was dry if not warm, wrapped his blanket twice around himself and drank Tennants Super to help him sleep, hugging Styler's warm body like a hot water bottle. Every now and then, when sure he was alone, Laramie took out the jewellery box, the five gold rings, looking them over with childish glee. He would sell them, he decided. The money would be his Christmas present to himself. He deserved it.

But when he attempted to pawn the rings, Laramie was turned away repeatedly. He had no ID, no receipt. Nobody would accept that the rings weren't stolen. He tried at least ten pawnshops in and around northwest London and the results were always the same. He had no friends. None of his acquaintances were any better off than him. Soon Laramie realised the truth – there was nobody he could sell the rings to.

A week passed, then two. Christmas came and went. Kensal Rise wasn't as kind to Laramie as Ladbroke Grove. People weren't as rich, so they didn't feel guilty about passing his blanket without dropping some change. He had no regulars, just random people who took him as another scrounger and told him to get a job, the usual stuff. By the second week in January he was camped out on his Ladbroke corner again, both he and Styler sitting keen-eyed, waiting; even looking in through the windows of the jewellery store when their patience wore thin. He never saw her.

One blustery evening when street signs danced like drug-filled teenagers and The Public walked with hoods and umbrellas, he noticed the spotty white kid locking up and decided he would ask after Blaine. He crossed the road and approached the kid, who saw him and tried to pretend he hadn't. Laramie ignored the hurried jangling of keys, refusing to be stung by the spotty kid's behaviour.

'Excuse me…'

A quick glance over one shoulder.

'Yeah, what's happenin', mate?'

He turned the lock and slipped the key into his jacket very self-consciously, already beginning to step away.

'I was jus' wonderin' why Blaine hasn't been in the last few days. Is she ill, or…'

The spotty kid looked at Laramie as though he was lower than a flea on Styler's paw, his cratered red face twisting into a wince of displeasure.

'Who wants to know?'

'Me innit?'

The kid puffed up his chest.

'And who are you?'

Laramie rolled his eyes.

'Larry. Does it make any difference? Can't you just tell me where she is?'

The kid looked him in the eye, cocky now. Laramie watched him preen and felt the urge to punch him. His eyes must have communicated at least some of his anger because all of a sudden the kid's chest fell along with his gaze and he looked small and weedy again, all spots and skinny limbs way too long for the rest of his body.

'She's probably at home where she belongs, mate. The boss give 'er the sack. She was stealin'.'

The wind picked up around them, blowing crisp packets and cans down All Saints Road. His mouth opened, to no avail.

'All right mate, be lucky...'

He was left on the corner with his dog, the jewellery box and guilt.

Laramie had once heard Ladbroke Grove described as a village, and though he judged this as pushing things a little too far, he felt it ought to be possible to find Blaine. He wandered the cold streets looking in every coffee shop and wine bar, scouring the fruit and veg stalls, the shoe shops – even, in a burst of inspiration, the local health clinic – but Blaine was nowhere to be found. He was sure she was a local – judging by the way she spoke, her accent and dress sense. Over time he grew less sure of his assumptions. Nevertheless, he continued to pace the streets.

A few days later everything happened in reverse. He was standing next to the underground public toilets by the Ground Floor Bar, chatting idly to the disabled guy with the harmonica and lazy Alsatian, when he felt arms wrap themselves around his waist, a head pressing against the small of his back. He heard his name called and every nerve in his body seemed to burst into life. He spun around, not quite believing it could be true and there she was, four Tesco's bags beside her, looking as cute and pretty as ever. He couldn't help launching himself at her, even as Styler pawed at her knees in excitement and Blaine giggled helplessly. The disabled guy and his dog watched, both feeling a little out of place. When the reunion finally died down Blaine insisted they follow her home.

He let Styler run free to nose in all the boxes and bins for dinner, whilst he took a couple of Blaine's shopping bags. They walked past the bright lights of the Electric Cinema, up the slight incline of Portobello Road. The young woman was bursting with hysterical joy.

'Where you bin, Larry, I was looking for you everywhere…'

In his excitement at finding her, the reason why they hadn't seen each other had fled his mind. It was strange, yet there seemed no change in her manner towards him; indeed, her initial greeting had been less like that of a friend and more like the way a woman would greet her lover. He didn't dare to think too much about it, but it seemed as though Blaine didn't know that he'd taken the box. He looked into her eyes, saw them sparkle and began to feel handsome again. It was good to be missed and wanted.

'I jus' had to leave the area… Christmas and all that shit… It was gettin' to me, man… I couldn't take it….'

'Well, you could've come to stay with me!' she exclaimed before he could finish. 'I got space and I spent Christmas on my own! We coulda spent it together, Larry. I needed the company, you'll see… You're so silly…'

Yes he was, Laramie agreed. Extremely silly. They reached the estate, a few blocks away from the market, walked inside and up damp concrete steps to the third floor. Laramie watched the curve of her rump still shifting, still very much apparent despite her long winter coat, and a longing he'd suppressed for so long he'd forgotten what it felt like consumed him in one huge gulp. The coat ensured that he could see nothing of her body, but it was easy to imagine the smooth butter of her ankles and calves leading to the firm bulk of her thighs, leading to…

The front door of her flat, painted in standard blue gloss paint, number 52 in silver metal above the letterbox. Laramie fought down the longing, feeling strong where he had once been weak.

'*Voila*,' Blaine sang, with a grin, putting her bags down and throwing her arms wide. 'Here's my castle!'

'Looks good…'

Laramie tried for enthusiasm but failed. Surprisingly, Blaine's grin only got wider. Then something in her face changed. A mist veiled her eyes and she moved towards him, until she was standing just below his chin. She leant forwards. Soft lips were on his before he knew it, pressing lightly before their warmth was gone. He stared at Blaine, her shopping bags still in his hands, not sure what to do.

'Bin wantin' to do that for ages,' she confessed, stroking his

cheek. He held back an urge to flinch, embarrassed by its roughness. 'Still wanna come inside?'

'Yeah…' he muttered.

Blaine went around the flat switching on lights and muttering
beneath her breath. Hers was the type of council flat Laramie had
seen a hundred times, a clone of scores he'd visited during his
lifetime. The hallway and kitchen walls were a dull white colour,
the living room a cross between terracotta and orange. There was
one shelf of about eight books above the TV. Most of the
furniture was recognisably Ikea. The TV and video were brands
he'd never heard of. Blaine offered him a seat on a bulky two-
seater sofa and disappeared from the room with the shopping
bags. He held onto Styler's lead, drawing comfort from her
weight against his foot, scratching her ears absently.

There was only one photograph in the room. Placed on top
of the TV, it looked like a studio photo of a much younger Blaine
holding a tiny red-faced baby caught mid-bawl. The young
woman was dressed up, wearing make-up and looking a little
like a mannequin; he only recognised her smile. Laramie
scratched Styler's ears harder. There were no children's books,
clothes, or toys. He sat back in the sofa just before Blaine
returned with two mugs of tea. She was wearing a polo neck
jumper and tight-fitting blue jeans, her slender body curving
like a racetrack. She sat down next to Laramie and crossed her
legs, exposing the fluffy bear slippers she'd exchanged for her
trainers. Laramie forced a chuckle.

'So…' Blaine was clearly nervous too. Her eyes were cast down
on her steaming mug, her slim fingers tapping the rim like a
typist. 'Where were you over Christmas?'

'Kensal Rise… Not far…'

'Did you go back to the shop at all?'

'Yeah…'

'So you heard about what happened?'

He shifted on the sofa. Styler lay on the floor with her head
between her paws, lazy eyes moving slow, following their conversation.

'The spotty kid told me somethin'…'

Blaine laughed aloud, almost spilling her tea in the process.

'Gavin? He's a fuckin' joker, man. What did he say? Nothing good I suppose; he don't like me anyway…'

'Not much… Jus' you'd bin sacked, dat's all. What happened?'

She gave a quieter laugh and told him how her boss had got back later that afternoon, looking a mixture of stressed out and relieved. His daughter had been knocked over by a car on the way to school. Although her injuries were quite minor considering, they were keeping her in the hospital for observation. He'd popped into the pawnshop on the way home to pick up some of her personal items. Satisfied that Blaine was coping well enough, he'd almost reached the door when he remembered the box of five gold baby rings left on the shop counter the night before (probably by Gavin, Blaine told Laramie wryly). In his rush to get to the hospital, her boss had forgotten about them. Did Blaine have any idea why they weren't on the counter where they'd been left?

A frantic search of the shop found nothing. Things got worse when the boss found out she'd stopped the surveillance video for close to three hours that afternoon. Blaine tried to tell him about the German tourists who'd packed the shop while the video was switched off, but without any evidence the boss hadn't believed her. She been sacked on the spot, made to pack her things and leave that instant. Blaine clutched her mug of tea tighter as she described how hard she'd cried, unsure whether she was being sacked for theft, or simple negligence. The pawnshop was her favourite job ever. Since then she'd heard nothing, though she had received her P45.

'So… What d'you think happened… to the box?'

She shrugged. 'It must have been the Germans innit? I think I remember seein' it, but there was so much goin' on I can't really remember for sure… They were the first customers we had, an' I know the box weren't on the counter when they left, so it must have been them… They wanted small stuff; easier to carry… They even said that… I'm so stupid…'

'No you're not.'

He reached out a hand and placed it on hers. Blaine's fingers were warm. She looked up, trying hard to smile, though the expression emerged as false as the story she'd woven, a story that left him out of the equation because she wished it so. Only now did he truly realise how deeply she felt for him – only now could he see the blessing he'd been given. For some reason he couldn't possibly begin to work out, Blaine thought she saw something special in him. He wanted to speak his realisation, empathise with her loss and tell her that he would be there for her from now until the end of his days; that nobody had treated him so kindly for many years and he guessed that nobody would. He wanted to say those things. Yet faced with this pretty woman in her rundown flat, jobless because of his actions, he couldn't say a word. Laramie stroked her hand and hoped that she could feel his sorrow, his regret, his new-found loyalty. From that moment onwards, he told himself, but only if she wanted him to, he would live his entire life for Blaine.

Laramie stroked her hand with a concentration that bordered on the obsessive. Styler looked annoyed by his switch of attention, grumbling a bit before eventually closing her eyes. Blaine gave another nervous giggle, and then took his hand and moved it slowly upwards to her breast. For a moment Laramie was frightened that this was only a dream, that he'd wake up on the hard pavement, one hand caressing Styler's teats. Blaine's intentions were unmistakeable as she lay back on the sofa with her eyes closed, the mug of tea still in one hand. She let him have his way with both breasts, murmuring quietly, legs writhing, head thrown back. After a while she sat up and put down the mug, removing his hand and dragging him to his feet. She led him to the bathroom. Dutiful as ever, Styler got up and followed.

'No girl, this is me an' Laramie time, no bitches allowed…'

Blaine shut the bathroom door on Styler. Laramie looked at the loofah, soaps and hair products, bewildered. A tall mirror was hooked to the back of the bathroom door. His face had the expression of a man who had witnessed his own ghost. Blaine was putting a plug in the tub, turning taps and pondering over the numerous bottles lined on the edge of the bath. All the while, Laramie stared. He looked more like a scarecrow than a human being. His red jacket was ripped and torn in many places. His trainers had splits so large his grimy socks were on display. Dark spots spread like shadows down the back of the arms, torso and hood. His beard wasn't as long as some he'd seen, though it still managed to obscure his face to a point where sallow yellow was hard to find. The few patches of skin on display were dry and pale.

Blaine was swishing her hand in the bath water trying to work up suds when she looked up, noticing Laramie's horror for the first time. She leapt up, sliding her body between Laramie and the mirror, pushing herself into his face in an attempt to get his attention back.

'OK, OK... Now you've seen the 'before', let's concentrate on 'after'. I'm a qualified beauty therapist, Larry; bet you didn't know dat did yuh? Did a two-year course an everythin'... I ain' got the equipment no more, but I can still do some stuff. By the time I've finished, you'll look like Pharell or one ah dem man, don't you worry, babe... You've got lovely skin, like butter or somefin'; it jus' needs some scrubbin', dat's all... I'll give you a wash, a shave, tweeze your ingrowing hair... You'll be clean enough to finish off what we started... Sound OK?'

He nodded silently, not wanted to speak in case he said something that would make her take it all back. Blaine was looking deep into his eyes, close enough to smell him even though she didn't react. Styler was scratching at the bathroom door. Blaine gave him a sultry smile.

'Two females fightin' for your attention tonight, Larry... You must feel pretty special innit...'

They laughed again; Laramie nervous now. She was scaring him and he didn't know why. Blaine closed in on him again; he almost backed away.

'People like you and me are survivors, Larry... We understand each other...' She took a deep breath, then looked him dead in the eye. 'I believe in Karma, Larry, an I believe Karma put you on dat corner for me to find you ... You look so much like Miguel...'

She laughed when she saw his puzzled look.

'*Miguel*... My baby father...' She choked on the words. 'I mean, the father of my child. I wouldn't say things was great between us but it hurt when he left me with Sandy... Couldn't take the screamin' he said... Well neither could bloody well I, but there was fuck all I could do about it, I had to take it didn't I? Serves us right for having kids young, dat's what most people would say and you know what? Part of me thinks they're right. Then... You know... I wasn't as capable as I might have been, left on me own with a kid, an' mum passed and no family you know, so Sandy... Sandy got ill an' the doctor said it was nobody's fault really, could've happened any time. I jus' should've got her to the hospital sooner. I told 'em I'd just waited cos I wasn't sure what to do... But I'd left her in the flat. Stupid innit? Not for dat long, jus' to see if I could get some tempin' work, only at the place on Goldbourne Road, what is it, twenny minutes walk from here to there? Anyway, I ended up being there all day an' when I got back Sandy was all still an' not movin' in the bottom of the cot like one of those dolls, you know, the ones that cry when you pick 'em up? When I did it though, she didn't make a peep an' dat's when I knew she was gone, but I ran down to the hospital anyway, I ran an' ran with Sandy in my arms... '

She broke down on her last few words, sobbing into his stinking jacket and beating on his chest as though he was the cause of her woe. Laramie wrapped his arms around her, more to ward her off than give comfort, trying not to smother her in his body odour. Blaine cried for quite a while. He wanted to feel pity, but all he could do was marvel at how fragile and weak she was compared with how tough she'd seemed on the streets. Get behind the doors and walls and you saw their traumas... Although they had houses and material possessions bought to ward off life's curses, their ills continued just the same.

Blaine sobbed until she couldn't cry any longer, pulling herself together bit by bit. Soon she was stone-faced, sniffling and puffing under her breath, her eyes dry and clear. Laramie was still standing on the same spot in the middle of the bathroom floor. She washed and dried her face, gave him a hug and proceeded to undress him, starting with the large red jacket.

He forced himself to relax, letting Blaine peel it from him without a word. It was only when she was finished and walking towards the bathroom door, and the weight of the box in his inner lining caused it to slam against the bath side, making a booming *thunk* sound that filled the room, that he remembered that under *no circumstances* was Blaine to ever lay hands on that jacket. He watched, screaming inside and yet strangely hesitant as she frowned, lifted it up, inspected the pocket, dug her hand inside, found the tear in the lining and retrieved what the jacket contained. She looked at the box for so long Laramie had time to come to the assumption – wild as it was – that her faith would remain rock solid and she'd dismiss what she'd found as a figment of an unstable mind. He made only one sound – an '*Uh*' that emerged more like an expression of resignation than a demand to stop. Blaine turned to face him, box in one hand, jacket in the other. Face churning like an earthquake, she hit him with both in the chest, the jacket obscuring his vision as her loud yell of anger finally arrived. A zipper or something must have caught his left eye, because suddenly he saw bright colours and he was blinded, holding his hand against his face to stem the pain, cursing as he felt Styler's breath all over him, her tongue on his hands.

He scrabbled around in a multicoloured whirl for a bit, then sat with his back resting against the side of the bathtub, waiting for the pain to subside. When it had, he felt gingerly at the swelling. Blaine was standing in the doorway. Her face was rigid. Fresh tears had reddened her eyes. She was holding a kitchen knife half-raised, glinting in the bathroom light.

'I want you out of my house… An' if you say one word, Larry, I won't be responsible for my actions… I jus' want you to shut up an' get out. Take the rings with you. I hope that they make you happy…'

Aching to protest, Laramie opened his mouth. Blaine's face contorted. She took a hurried step into the room, raising the knife.

'Don't give me an' excuse! Jus'… Go …' Now she sounded tired, world-weary. 'Jus' go, Laramie… Please…'

He picked up the box and grabbed Styler's lead, tugging her past the tearful girl.

Things went back to dull regularity. Laramie camped out on his corner spot during the day, walking back to the building site on Kensal Rise before the sun went down. Six weeks later, some kids were using the site as a late-night place to explore and smoke weed when they happened on his sleeping body. They repeatedly stabbed the dog when it bit one of them, and beat Laramie until he was unconscious. When he came to the rings were gone. Styler had long bled to death beside him, her blood fanned out around her. Next morning, paler than ever, stumbling and squinting, Laramie gathered his blanket and left the building site, disappearing into the mass of morning commuters.

FLIGHT OF FREEDOM

His first inkling that something strange was happening came when he noticed an annoying itch on both shoulder blades. He, of course, was Marcus Jennings, your lower than average rude boy type who lived in the heart of the Inner City – you know, the type of kid Ali G made millions parodying. And the itch? Well, the itch was nothing special at the time. Not painful but deep, insistent. Not nagging for attention but whining softly like a puppy left outside. He noticed it most in the mornings, but found when he left the house and went outside, got into conversation with the mans dem in their usual spot, he could ignore the itch. Smoking weed and drinking Nigerian Guinness also helped. And as they stood on the corner and bus' jokes and sold overpriced skunk to the tourists and complained about the gentrification of what they had once known and loved, he forgot that he'd ever had itchy shoulder blades. Until he left the corner for his tower block home.

There, with his head spinning and only thick darkness to gaze at, the itch came back with a vengeance that had him rubbing his back furiously against his mattress, making it impossible for him to sleep. Unable to quiet the sensation, he had taken to marching into the bathroom, grabbing his loofah and attacking his blades until his skin was tender. He only stopped because the pain grew stronger than the itch had been. He downed two aspirins, smoked some skunk and prayed he'd drift away.

Two days later he went to see his GP, Dr. McBride, after it became clear that the itch wasn't going away. The doctor gave him a routine check up, took his blood pressure, gazed into his eyes with his little torch thingy, then pronounced that Marcus was in perfect health. He'd have to go to St. Mary's for further blood tests, but the doctor was pretty sure there was nothing to worry about really. He felt around his shoulder blades when Marcus complained of feeling sore, putting the tenderness down to all the scratching. On a whim borne mainly out of the fact that he was completely baffled by Marcus's so called 'ailment', the GP placed his stethoscope on the shoulder blades, shrugged at his patient (who was giving him a very strange look), then inserted his earpiece and listened.

Later, Dr. McBride told his wife that what he'd heard was the strangest thing he'd come across in twenty years of medicine. Low-pitched, steady crunching sounds, the kind of sound he imagined cornflakes would make if you took a handful and crushed them in your fist. It took all of his experience and training to keep his face neutral, not to panic when he heard those noises. *Why didn't you just tell him?* Mrs. McBride had asked her husband. *I don't know – I just froze*, the doctor replied, looking at the floor, while his conscience reminded him, once again, that he was lying. He hadn't told Marcus because he didn't have a clue what was causing the noises, it was as simple as that. To admit that he didn't know something was near impossible for a man like him who always knew *everything*. So, the pride of Dr. McBride – excuse the lame rhyme, I couldn't resist – saved Marcus from becoming some kind of medical oddity for the remainder of his natural life.

As did the fact that Marcus never went for his blood tests. He had suspected something was badly wrong when the itching refused to go away, even more when he saw McBride's rigid, emotionless mask as he held the cold stethoscope and listened. Intuition told him the doctor was hiding something. Which probably meant that what he had was very bad, maybe even terminal. Marcus went straight home that day, avoiding his usual corner with his usual bredrins, instead stopping off at the local Tesco's Express to buy as much provisions as he could afford. If he was going to die, he would go out with a bang. He would experience everything that he'd ever dreamed about.

Up until that point, Marcus had been a bit of a nonstarter. He'd been average at school, far too average to be interested in college, opting for the brighter allure of street life. He'd tried selling various drugs, only to realise you had to be more than average at maths in order to make it worthwhile; and he was not. When he turned and looked around it had been ten years since he'd left school. He hadn't managed to gain anywhere near the amount of money it took to have the cars, women and respect drugs were supposed to bring. He fell back on his giro, which meant that although he was handsome, he stopped attracting the type of women he dreamed of. As his confidence plummeted, he stopped attracting any at all. These days he stood on the corner selling the odd draw for other dealers, turning ten-pound bags into twenty and nicking a spliff in the bargain. Sometimes he remembered his dreams of being someone big as he stood with all the others pretending that they did this only to keep their area real, to prove that they were still as hardcore and street as ever. The lie had never held much weight for Marcus. He still wanted something other than the life he'd been awarded, but, much like his itch, he tried to pretend the feeling never existed.

The itch soon gave way to a pain that had him running to the 24-hour store in the early hours of the morning, buying 6 packets of painkillers, going through three by the following night. Over the next week, sleep became a thought dreaded almost as much as death. He could not do it on his back. He turned onto his side and stomach, wincing in pain whenever he forgot and rolled over. Though the drugs dulled his agony into a low-level hum, like the song says, they didn't quite work.

One morning, after going through the worst night of the lot, falling asleep only from sheer exhaustion, he opened his eyes to feel... Nothing. The pain was gone. Yeah, he felt a little sore and tender but that was minor compared to the howling agony he'd been forced to endure until now. Stunned, not quite believing his troubles had disappeared, he crept towards his full-length mirror, and looked over his left shoulder.

There, reflected just below his incredulous face and the muscles of his neck, was a tiny, damp wing. It was slightly bent over, limp as a plant's new shoot. It smelt musty, probably due to the wet feathers. The top half, the half nearest his chin was grey, though the colouring faded to creamy white at the tip. Trembling, Marcus turned his head to the right and saw its identical twin. He wondered if they would move. As he wondered this, they flapped weakly in response. He gasped, tried again, laughing as it worked. It was as easy as moving his arm, or fingers. Joy flowed through him until he was jumping on the spot, grinning from ear to ear, whooping loudly.

I've got wings, he kept whispering under his breath, *Surely that means I can fly!*

He didn't know how this miracle had happened, but if he was going to fly, he obviously couldn't do it with those weaklings on his back. He'd have to wait. Wait and see what happened.

It took twelve days for the weaklings to become strong, twelve days in which he continued avoiding the friends and dealers he'd once seen on a daily basis, even though they often came by his flat, demanding he let them in. Marcus refused. It wasn't that he was ashamed of his new body parts – far from it – but he knew as well as anyone what the manor was like. Once a person had wings, everyone else would want them, wouldn't they? First, he'd be inundated with questions: *How did you get them, what did you do, how could I get them?* Then, when people realised he didn't know and couldn't help, admiration would turn to jealousy. If he reacted badly, that would be it. They'd seek a way to deal with him. That would definitely involve violence of some kind.

So Marcus hid.

That didn't mean he stayed away from everyone. Some nights he put on a raincoat and headed for the nearest park. When he got there, he took of the coat to reveal his bare torso, stretching his wings to the fullest. The only people in the park at that time were lovers (straight and gay), and all were amazed by his mutation. Each wing was two feet long by that time, growing stronger every day. Sometimes he'd flap hard enough to levitate a foot or so, though this brought a return of the pain and he didn't do it often. On every visit to the park the pain would lessen a fraction. At the end of the second week, it was gone. One night, two Italian girls strolled past hand-in-hand, making a beeline for him. They'd heard, they told him. They were wondering… Did he have any other amazing body parts?

His secret was out. After the night with the Italian girls, he'd been so pleased with himself he walked home from the park with his growing limbs on display for all to see. He hadn't gone far

74

before a car steamed past, packed with four of the guys that he used to move with. Even though he'd known it was coming, the depth of their aggression still shocked him. They screamed, jeered and threw cans. Marcus didn't bother with a reply, flexing his angel-like wings. They were past six feet now, one of his park admirers had told him. If he wanted to get away from all he'd known, now was the time.

As he walked into his tower block lobby, stunning the security guard into a near fit, he knew they'd wait until he got inside his flat before they came. He had time. Once inside, he packed a small gym bag with essential items – his passport (he laughed at the sight of the little burgundy booklet, but took it anyway), a few clothes, a toothbrush, what little money he had and some favourite CDs. Then he opened his patio doors onto the outside world.

His flat was on the 14th floor of Trellick Towers. The tallest council block in Europe, let alone London. He'd been thinking about jumping since that first morning he looked in the mirror, but had been too scared he might fall. Now, as he stared over his shoulders at the feathery appendages, there was only anticipation – only joy. He could do it. He knew that he could, believed that he could. And if he couldn't, what else was there? Resign himself to a life where he had wings, but couldn't use them? A life as a chicken instead of an eagle?

He climbed on the ledge and perched. When the shouting came he closed his eyes and relished the noise. It was the sound of victory, the sound of deliverance. There was pounding on the door, the steady thud of boots, a crash and harsh breathing as they tumbled inside. He waited until he heard them catch sight of him.

Without opening his eyes, he let himself go.

There was an instant rush of wind in his ears and the sound of his former friends' screams of shock, which eventually faded until all he could hear was the rapid beat of his heart. He waited as long as he could before he tilted the wings, his stomach churning in response as he levelled out, and then climbed. Marcus opened his eyes to see the city – *his city* – new, fresh, alive. He imagined seeing the unexplored world beyond West London. A smile came to his lips.

HIS HEALING HANDS

1

Memories lay like a stack of cards to be shuffled and dealt subconsciously, needing no will to play them. Filling his brain, surging through his nerves, creating anger, sadness, joy... each one a suite of emotions that marked his mood. All had something in common. All were coloured by something that made their worth equal.

All had the taint of the gift.

The sun beamed in through the window, creating a path of light and dust motes. In the flat below, the lady who was usually screaming '*Go to school!*' at her kids was silent. Passing cars made the only sound on the streets outside. Today was different. There was no way to put a finger on what it was, but it was different. That was for sure.

The air was sensual, pregnant with summer and heat that rose slowly. The trees outside the house had burst into oyster-pink flowers that the breeze rustled and blew onto the pavement. That wasn't the reason things had changed. The seasons would come and go, but the difference inside would remain.

A full deck lay before him, the cards fanned out in his mind's eye.

He picked one at random and turned it face up.

The sun was blazing that day, too, but the heat was heavy – a weight that seemed to press the boy's sweaty head deep into his shoulders. He could hardly get the Cola ice-pole he was holding into his mouth – this was because he was holding his father's left hand and walking at a pace that was making his arm jerk like a puppet. He had no idea where they were going in such a hurry. The ice-pole slipped from his numb fingers and shattered into black crystals on the pavement. He pointed at its remains, distraught.

'Nevah min' dat. Come.'

Ignoring his squeal of indignation, his father walked on. Dryness filled the boy's mouth. Their pace didn't slow until they stood before the front door. His father pressed the bell and waited, tense.

'Do yuh bes' yuh 'ear? Do yuh bes'.'

The boy didn't reply. His father pushed his head with his fingertips. He nodded, silent, without looking up. The boy's thoughts were still on the ice-pole, the way it had shattered on the ground. Like glass, brittle, fragile and sharp. The front door opened. The boy looked up, found himself under the massive shadow of Flinty's belly. Before Flinty could say a word, his father pushed his son even closer, mocking the other man.

'Ready to lose money, Dragon Belly?'

The man held up his hands in protest.

'Yuh mus' stop dis stupidness, Gypsy. Dis ain' right!' Flinty blazed. The boy's father took no notice, simply gunning down Flinty's defences. When the man had no arguments left, he was still there. Realising resistance was useless, Flinty let them in.

The house was dark and moody; mixed odours hung in the air. The boy could feel the sickness stifling his nose, making his head ache with instant pain. As they were led up stairs littered with piles of clothes, the strength of the sickness increased, radiating from somewhere above. Flinty took them along another passage, then stood outside a thick mahogany door with a crystal doorknob that shone like a diamond. The boy remembered the last time this had happened – a month ago, but it seemed a lifetime. He'd healed an old drinking buddy of his father's. Gypsy had won fifty pounds from his gift that time. Fright leapt into his body, but it was too late. He was pushed into the room, the door was shut, a key turned behind him. He banged loud with tears in his eyes until he heard the breathing.

The boy turned. His eyes widened as he spied the room's occupant. An old woman, twice the size and width of Flinty, with bare arms so huge you could see the fat beneath flesh. Her laboured breathing was painful to hear. Chest rising in fits and starts, body rattling and shaking like a broken down car. A huge leg protruded from beneath the duvet. There was a thick stench in the air, making it hard to breathe.

The boy watched in horror, a scream starting from the base of his throat, rising until he felt that he could no longer hold it back. Then something else took control. Instinct flooded his being, flushing out doubt. He knew what to do. It only had to be done.

Inner calm overtook him, erasing panic. He walked to the bed in a trance, putting all his strength into lifting the leg. When that was done he walked over to where her head lay. The face was kindly, despite the rigours the body was going through, etched with time and other things the boy knew nothing of. He placed his hands on the woman's forehead. It was cool and firm, something like marble to the touch. She didn't stir. He wondered what was wrong with her. Pity flooded him. He closed his eyes.

He imagined the woman breathing without effort again in this house. The walls and windows were gleaming with life and light. He imagined her smiling and hugging Flinty, her face filled a rich brown instead of dusky grey. He imagined her happy.

He placed his hands on her chest, stomach, ankles. When he was done he looked at her with a smile. Her chest still rose fitfully, though the shaking in her body was gone. It would take some time but eventually she'd be all right. He didn't know how he knew this, but he knew he was right. He knocked to be let out of the room.

His watch said he'd been there almost forty-five minutes. Still smiling, he left the healing woman to recover.

He knew she was better two weeks later when Flinty came to the house in tears. As well as his father's money, Flinty brought an extra hundred for him – no mean feat at the time, even for someone of his means. He also brought the biggest bag of sweets, crisps, chocolate and nuts the boy had ever seen in his life. His father let him keep the snacks, but took the hundred pounds and put it in a secret place for when he was older.

He'd been ten at that time. By the age of eighteen the whole world seemed to know. Well, the whole of Grove anyway. Everything happened here, didn't it? Everything that mattered to him. He loved the notoriety and the curiosity it brought, even if his father didn't. He loved the way the girls talked about him and the way brers listened to what he had to say on any given subject. His gift was known and accepted as a part of his make-up, just like his skinny frame and coolie hair. It made him money and gave him unlimited respect. Why wouldn't he want to harbour a thing like that?

At eighteen he was a healer by trade, not by force. Word of mouth rather than his father's boasts and bets recommended him. He chose whom he wanted to lay his hands on and paid rent to live in a spare room at a school friend's house, meals and other bills included. His life was his own.

One morning he arrived at the house of a boy who'd asked him to visit, saying he'd been born with crippling asthma that made breathing near impossible. He was pleasantly surprised when a girl he recognised from around opened the door. Her name was Shanique, the *que* said like a K. He knew this because he'd heard a lot of the brers talking about her. Shanique was *the lick, live, slammin', fit, buff*… adjectives that failed to measure the young woman in the flesh.

She held the door open. He went in. He asked her where the patient was; she told him upstairs. He followed her into a girl's room, full of posters, clothes and beauty products. He turned and stared at her in his relaxed way.

'Where's the patient?'

'There isn't one.'

She smiled and closed the door behind her, turning the key. A thousand childhood memories resurfaced. He forced them down, made them be quiet.

'What about the person who made the call?'

She giggled in a manner that was a little sly.

'That was my brother. He's not sick. He was lying for me.'

She crossed the room and stood in front of him. He got it now – of course he got it – he was quiet, not stupid. It was surprise that knocked the words from his mouth like a schoolyard bully. The only question was why she'd chosen him. She'd always seemed to have plenty of admirers while he'd ignored her existence, his mind on Mrs. Cain's bunions, or Mr. May's broken leg. Now she was right in front of him, he couldn't deny her presence any more. He could smell her fragrance, see her body and hear her voice.

'Well pleased to meet you anyhow,' he grinned back.

She laughed. The instinct came to him once again when he heard that sound. He knew that today was the day; *she* was the reason why he'd held back from the others. Although he was glad it was so, he was also a little afraid. He believed that over time, he'd trained himself to be a better healer. He was surer in his work, quicker to diagnose, faster to heal. What nagged at him was the thought that his life was preordained to some degree. It meant he had no control over what could, or should happen to him.

Shanique's ebony eyes urged him to trust her. He had to rely on instinct to lead him in the right direction.

'So I heard about you an' Terri. How come you split up?'

He shrugged, unable to put his new ideas into words so soon.

'She told me you didn't even–' she paused. 'You know – why not?'

He let his shoulders rise and fall again.

'You ain' gay are you? It'd be the livin' waste…'

He sighed in disbelief and tried to go for the door. She stood before it, arms outstretched in a classic pose. She knew he wouldn't touch her and so did he. She smiled with so much charm he was forced to return the expression.

'Don't be offended. I had to ask. Terri's so pretty an' dat…'

'She's beautiful,' he admitted, reluctantly. He knew this was a road that could lead to trouble.

'So what about me?' she returned, confirming his fear. 'Am I beautiful?'

He laughed. 'Shanique, you know the answer to that–'

'Dat's not what I meant. I wanna hear what you think.'

He rubbed his shaven head while she stood there smiling. He wanted to leave, but knew he wouldn't, couldn't. Wasn't there always free will? The side of him that said there was found itself galled by the knowledge that instinct provided. Even as Shanique grinned, he wondered how much her actions were guided by something outside her, some destiny. A few minutes ago he would have claimed that her plans were being driven by the most basic of human urges. Now he wasn't so sure, for her smile said differently. Her smile said she knew as much as he.

'Come.'

She walked to the bed without looking back. At that point he gave up, felt his penis stir. She sat down and patted the duvet. He obeyed, as pliant as a child's action figure. She put a hand on his leg and he saw it was trembling. For the first time he noticed how nervous she was.

'You're shaking.'

'You're makin' me shake.'

He smiled at that, touched her black hair. Their eyes met, the attraction too strong for them to part. He leaned into the softness of her lips, probing with his tongue, nibbling with his teeth, liking the way she tasted, the way she rubbed his chest. He bit the nape of her neck and she moaned. Their breathing came in short bursts. They stripped without delay.

A lull inserted itself into their passion. Now they sat on the bed opposite each other, running light fingers over nipples, bellies, thighs. He let out an involuntary sigh when her nails skimmed his penis; other than that, neither made a sound. He licked his own thumb, stroked her clit as gently as a mouse until she came. When her excitement died they lay back on the bed.

'I waited fuh you,' she told him, dark eyes glowing like onyx.

'Same goes for me,' he replied, though he'd only just realised this.

'I don't want us to have sex. I want us to make love. Can you do that?'

He nodded in earnest and meant it, giving in to fate's pull.

Another card, another time; almost another life. Four years came and passed, with Shanique firmly at his side. She was his best friend, his constant ally; arguments between them were rare. They moved in together when they both reached twenty-one, blessed with the consent of Shanique's parents. He looked forward to every day, apart from September 16th, the day of his father's birth and death.

Each year he made the arduous journey to Kensal Green cemetery, growing more reluctant with each visit. His father had died when he was fourteen. As he had no mother, he'd been taken into care immediately, though the loss hadn't made much difference to his childhood. Gypsy had never been the most attentive of fathers, preferring a night out with his drinking partners to one indoors with his child, who was usually left home with whomever his father was sleeping with at the time. He only paid the boy mind when someone needed healing. He charged patients ample sums and never gave his son one penny. His attentions were rare, brief, and only vaguely anything to do with love.

Once, as he was getting dressed for his annual journey, Shanique asked to come along. He agreed without a second thought; it was only when they were walking alongside the high cemetery wall that enclosed the grounds that he began to feel uneasy. Shanique was chatty and full of wit, though she watched him carefully. His pace slowed. He grew serious and quiet, holding her fingers with his free hand as they passed the cemetery entrance. An old man on the gate waved in recognition. He waved back with the hand that was holding the bouquet – then looked at the flowers as if acutely embarrassed, and quickened his pace.

The hot sun made the gravestones gleam. They wandered amongst other roaming mourners, sometimes saying hello, sometimes acting as if they were in a separate world. He led, Shanique followed, watching his expression grow harder with each step until they finally came to a large headstone of black granite flecked with gold. Engraved in gold, the inscription told them that this was the grave of Robert 'Gypsy' Kweli; 'An Honourable Man'. Shanique stood still as he walked to the grave and laid down his flowers. He knelt on the grass, staring in the direction of the headstone.

He felt caught in a whirlpool of feelings. Outside, he was as much granite as the severed piece of rock in front of him; inside, he felt liquid, mushy like rotten fruit. Up until the age of eight he had loved his father dearly, though that feeling had always come mixed with a healthy dose of fear. In his early teenage years, the hate had begun to rise and he'd lost count of the times he wished Gypsy dead. Now, here he was, all his pillow-soaked boyhood dreams realised, that one dark wish thrust aggressively into the bright summer day. He couldn't remember ever hugging the body beneath the earth, or even touching the soul that had fled to who knew where.

Thinking these once-a-year thoughts, he was surprised by cool fingers on his neck. He jumped and turned. Shanique kissed him on his temple, knelt down on the grass beside him, kneading his shoulder and neck with strong fingers.

'Let it go.'

He frowned at her.

'Huh?'

'Let it go. It's OK to admit you loved him.'

He moved away from her.

'I know. I don't need *you* to say that.'

'No, you don't know. You're always pretending you were such good mates. He was never around but you understood cos you were such good mates. Being good mates is fine; that's your *father* down there. You're acting as if it was some bloke you kicked a football around with.'

'Are you telling me how to grieve?'

The distance between them had grown. She closed the space and held his hand again.

'*No*. It's just that I see this distance you've created and that's fine if that how you really feel. But I think I know you by now and I think it'd be good for you to let go. All that pent-up hurt inside'll kill you if you let it. Admit your feelings, be honest with yourself, get it out of your system…'

He opened his mouth to speak but the words stuck in his throat. His eyes began to well with tears. He looked at the grass, but she lifted his chin with a finger, telling him it was OK, it was allowed, let it out. He gulped hard in an attempt to force them back and they ran down his cheeks regardless. Abandoning his attempts to stem their flow, he hugged Shanique tight, thinking that for once, he was the one who'd been healed.

He laid down his cards when he heard a key in the door, sitting up on his bed. So much told him it was her – the way the door slammed, the way she sighed when it was shut – all of those things provided irrefutable ID. Shanique rushed into the bedroom in panic, so he knew that he'd scared her with his call. She stood in the doorway and stared when she saw him fully clothed and sitting up.

'What happened?'

He shrugged. 'I'm not sick or anything like that; at least I don't think so. I feel pretty normal apart from this weird feeling in my bones.'

'They told me it was an emergency at work. Then I phoned here and I got a disconnected tone. What's goin' on?'

'I pulled out the phone wire. I didn't want any calls for bookings.'

Her emotions filled the air; he knew she was confused and scared. He wasn't helping matters, but this wasn't easy for him either. She tried to work it out for herself, going back over the evidence.

'Wha's dis about a mad feelin' in yuh bones?' she asked. He looked up and grabbed her hand, played with her fingers.

'Siddown, Shanique. I gotta chat to you.'

He felt the bedsprings contract under her weight, felt the warmth of her body next to his. All at once he needed that contact, so he moved close and put an arm around her. She looked at him, scared now, so he kissed her and rubbed her shoulder with his right hand.

'It's gone, Shanique. I can't do it any more.'

She made as if to ask *what* – then she realised and her mouth gaped open.

'*Can't* – or won't? D'you mean you're givin' up?'

'Can't. I knew it the moment I woke up.'

He explained it to her – the feeling of loss, of something missing, detached, severed – no matter the word, it couldn't hold the weight of what had happened. He told her how he'd wandered around the flat distraught; how he'd cried, screamed, roared – all in vain.

'Yuh still don't know it's really gone,' she argued. 'Your feelin's could be nuttin' more than paranoia.'

He showed her the cut on his hand. It was a large and gaping, dry prickles of torn skin marking the edge of the wound, the inside red and raw. She gasped when she saw it, grabbing his wrist, pulling his arm closer to her face.

'Where the hell did dat come from?'

'I did it. To see if I could heal myself. As you can see, I couldn't. That's how I knew it was gone…'

She put his head against her shoulder and wept into his hair. They shuddered and whimpered together on the bed.

Three months passed. Three months that were not easy. He struggled to come to terms with the fact that his healing days were over, while Shanique weathered his temper, fits of depression and bouts of tears. At twenty-three years old he found himself signing on for the first time in his life and he barely endured the embarrassment. News of his loss had spread through the community like flu. Everybody knew; most also signed on. Every fortnight he confronted the inquisitive faces of those who were concerned, the amused smirks of those who had been jealous, and questions, questions, questions… He took the first job he could find, a sales assistant in a local Blockbuster. That was just as bad; everyone he knew rented dvds too. He gave up that job within two weeks.

Stuck within the four walls of his flat, the acute boredom almost drove him mad. He'd never been much of a loafer, and he didn't smoke or drink. There was no one he could visit; all his friends worked. The void made by the loss of his healing seemed bottomless, vast and dark. There were times when suicide was a serious option.

His love for Shanique was the only thing that stood between him and eternal night. Even in his dreams, she was a never-ending source of salvation. If he was drowning, she was a sleek brown seal come to rescue him; if flames trapped him, she called on the spirits and conjured a cloud filled with rain. In his waking moments Shanique was a great deal less grand in her efforts to comfort him, but he couldn't have managed without her there. Though something inside him had altered, she hadn't – and it proved she *wouldn't*. This meant more than any feats his dreams could create.

Spring had almost passed when Shanique came home from work and hugged him so tight he almost suffocated. She kissed him, led him into the bedroom and sat him down. He was peering at her through the glasses he now wore to watch TV.

'I wanned to tell you dis right *here*, for old time's sake.'

He prompted her with a slight frown, along with the quizzical half-smile on his lips.

'Feel my belly. What's underneath?'

Still frowning, he did as he was asked – then instinct hit him again for the first time in months and he knew what she was saying. Looking up into her eyes, he saw that she was breathing fast, excited. She put her hand over his and nodded.

He closed his eyes in joy so exquisite it hurt.

'How many months?' he asked, barely managing the words.

'Three,' she told him, watching his face as he counted – nodding her head once more when his wide eyes met hers. Three months ago he'd thought that something had been lost, had died. Now he found that something had merely moved on, been reborn.

'It'll be a girl,' he said to Shanique, feeling as sure as the moment of their first kiss.

'I know,' she replied.

THE CHILD WHO WISHED

Each step across the bustling school playground was an exercise in torture for the child. He walked, head held high, eyes fixed on some vague spot, lips trembling but refusing to cry as the teacher guided him through playing children. The hand on his shoulder was apparently there for comfort. Ebi understood this as a substitute for her reassurances back inside the building, kind words laced with a never-quite-voiced apology. Only minutes ago she'd knelt before him, engaging Ebi with wide blue eyes, hands constantly pushing wispy hair away from her face, speaking the words slow and clear, attempting to make him understand. The school corridor had been quiet, with only a distant hum of young voices accompanied by the louder bark of teachers. Despite her efforts, Ebi heard nothing beyond an unspoken desire for forgiveness. The smell of polished wood, not unlike the stench of vomit, assaulted his nostrils, making his stomach churn.

Then the hand was on his shoulder, forcing him down stairs, through doors and back towards the place that he dreaded most – the playground – surrounded by a sea of unfamiliar faces flowing back and forth. Ebi caught still photos of animated features, staring, shouting, screaming more of those unintelligible words, their force and power driving him stumbling back into the legs of the teacher. The hand on Ebi's shoulder tightened. He heard her speak down to him again, her high-pitched voice almost drowned by the roar of the four hundred children his mother had told him attended this school; 'Together with you, that makes four hundred and one!' she'd smiled as she dressed him that first morning.

They walked as far as the playground perimeter. Ebi stood with his back firm against the wooden fence, watching the expressions of children immersed in various games, recognising only hopscotch, tag and football. The weight on his shoulder disappeared and the hand was gone. His teacher knelt before him once again, whispering another strange collection of foreign words. She stood up, smiling in sympathy, walking away. Before Ebi could blink, she was swallowed by the mass animal of dancing, swirling children that rose up as one and ate her whole.

Their noise was a steady roar in his ears, one sustained note. He moved backwards until his spine was rubbing hard against the wooden fence, eyes beginning to burn and flutter. Tears were just below the surface, glistening like jewellery. He was afraid to look up, afraid to wish, almost afraid to breathe. Children ran back and forth; sometimes close enough for their skin to brush against his. None spoke to Ebi.

He wanted to be brave, just as his mother had asked; yet he felt his head falling until he was gazing at the speckled grey of gravel. The mottled colour reminded him of their birds, not quite white and very far from black. At home, stone could be found in myriad colours… Vibrant reds, sparkling oranges, sandy beige… Sometimes they contained white wisps like faraway clouds, even two colours merged into one. The land was warm, almost alive. Ebi had never seen anything like this colourless rock beneath his feet that looked sapped of life, just like the sky. Ebi knelt to touch rough, uneven concrete. He closed his eyes and laid his palm flat, absorbing the unyielding surface, wishing that one out of the four hundred would talk to him just this once.

A moment later a body careered into his, slamming him back against the playground fence. He gasped as wind was knocked from his body. Ebi waited a moment, sure their roughness was just a mistake. He opened his eyes, his smile of success shrinking into nothing when he saw the three boys united by matching grins.

'All right, Jungle Boy?'

That was the one that had bumped him. Lance. He was the tallest of the three, lanky and grim. One of the others had a matching meanness, though he lost fair and square where height was concerned. This was Nathan. The third was a curiosity that

Ebi had never seen before. A child with an uncombed ginger Afro, light skin and brown freckles that dotted his face as though they'd been painted on. As if this wasn't enough to make him stand out, the curiosity's name was Fox. Ebi had already been told that this wasn't a nickname; Fox's parents had christened him that way. He knew this because the three boys were notorious throughout Stanworth Primary School. As Ebi's mother had explained the first time, every school had a bully; even the best school in the country had at least one. Ebi wondered if that made Stanworth Primary pretty exceptional; one small building with two floors, and yet here he was, faced with not one, not two, but three school bullies! If he could stand their taunts, surely he would do well.

Ebi didn't answer. This was partly because Lance made no sense and partly because the look on their faces had informed him of their intentions. His eyes began to sting again. Ebi felt tiny, and the world seemed a great deal darker, as if their skinny, scabbed bodies had blocked the sun. They moved in on him until there seemed no escape. Their words came faster, often accompanied by flecks of spittle, which gathered at the corners of their mouths. He flinched as those random droplets landed on his arms, legs and sometimes, most horribly, his face. Whenever they said something, the boys would take turns to push him back against the hard wooden fence.

'Jungle boy.'

'Go back home.'

'Why don't you learn to speak our language, you monkey?'

'Dirty African.'

'Go home.'

'Stinkin' African.'

When they tired of looking mean, the fists began to fall. Ebi crouched, trying to protect his head as he felt feet land on his thighs and back. With a roar he sprang like a lion, throwing wild punches without looking. He caught one, he didn't know whom, then the others grabbed his arms and held him down. When his blind rage cleared he realised that the one he'd hit was Lance. He stood before him holding his split lip. The look in his eyes scared Ebi to the bone; though just a child, Lance had the feverish look of the village wild dogs that lay in the heat all day, then ran around biting anyone who came near. Entranced, wide-eyed as he noticed how many children had gathered to watch, all Ebi's resistance fled. He was slumped long before the punches connected with his cheeks, lips and eyes. Was deaf to the cries of his surrounding audience. They ripped his school shirt and bloodied his face, but still Lance, Nathan and Fox continued the beating.

Despite his teacher's kind words, Ebi found no rescue or reprieve. His torment ended only when they grew bored of their game, leaving him lying on the mottled concrete, dribbling red spittle between dark cracks in the gravel. Though in pain, he lay in a position that made it impossible for him not to watch their brown legs join the multicoloured forest of others, just as his teacher burst through the crowd of gathered children, red spots of anger highlighting her porcelain cheeks.

She walked him home that evening. Ebi could tell she was still indignant, or maybe even ashamed, because the red flowers were still in bloom on each cheek and this time she held his hand in hers instead of placing it on his shoulder. Her fingers were soft and damp, enclosing his fist in a warm cocoon of flesh, smothering his smaller hand. Ebi had been scared that they might see some of the other children on the way, but when he had eventually emerged from the School Nurse's office sometime later that afternoon, he'd found the corridors still and empty. As they walked the long high road, Ebi marvelled at everything going on: the postman with his bright red van collecting letters; the queue of elders forming a white-haired line out of the post office door; the sweet shop man having a friendly chat with the man from the fruit and veg store (Ebi staring in awe at what he'd imagined impossible); the HGVs, double-decker buses and vans creating a growl that far surpassed the mass voice of the playground. While his teacher led him through all this without even a glance, Ebi soaked up the tableau as though he could find the answer to all his problems within the noisy swoosh of the dual carriageway. The vehicles roared like a continual river of traffic. Ebi walked its banks, mindful of the power he saw.

When they reached his home, his mother was waiting at the

front door, telling him in Igbo that she had left work early to see what the monsters had done, that she would never allow it to happen again. She wailed and lamented, the teacher trying to calm her, the twin blooms spreading over her face, and it was only when Ebi approached them both, laying a hand on his mother's shoulder and saying, '*Nnem ha egbu beghi nu,*' – 'My mother, they haven't killed me!' – that she finally included him in her grief, grabbing him to her breast and wailing joy at the sight of his strength. The teacher stood back and let them console each other. Ebi was then taken upstairs to his tiny, well-ordered room while the two women talked. Over an hour later his teacher knocked on his bedroom door. She clasped his hand again, whispered words that he could only imagine meant goodnight and left their home.

They ate eba and egusi soup for dinner that night. His favourite meal. Afterwards, his mother bathed and re-bandaged his cuts and bruises with shea butter; she didn't trust whatever concoction the school nurse used. She sang to him while she worked, songs of brave young men like himself who never let the fight defeat them, always struggling onwards to eventual victory. Ebi sang along with her sometimes, closing his eyes and trying to use the words to conjure a feeling of home. But it was no use. Home was far behind him now, miles across a shimmering ocean he almost wished he could recross – but not quite. Ebi had wished to be with his mother and now here he was. He had never attempted to go back on a wish before. He wasn't even sure if that were possible; even if it were, wishing himself away from his mother was something he could never do.

He had been wishing for some time now. His mother told anyone who would listen of how he had been born with a pale skin that obscured his eyes, nose and mouth. The midwife had even thought he might be horribly disfigured until she probed further, soon realising the featureless mask was not fixed to his face. His mother often described the joy she had felt when the thin layer slipped away to reveal the handsome boy beneath. The midwife predicted that Ebi had been blessed with second sight; that he was a child whom the Gods favoured and as such he should be watched carefully. His father, ever the cynical businessman, dismissed her claims as nonsense. Although his mother liked the idea of Ebi being special, and would repeat the story emphatically as he'd grown ever older, the midwife's prophecy held no more prominence in her life than a child's fairy tale.

Nevertheless, the belief took firm root. The Gods had given him power. Ebi would put it to use.

Alone in the darkness of his bedroom, Ebi remembered lying in almost the same position at home, six months before, his thoughts projected into the impenetrable blackness of the ceiling, wishing he could be with his mother in the faraway land of England. It had been his biggest wish to date; up until then, wishes had been confined to the little things in life: candy, a new toy at Christmas, eba and egusi soup for dinner every week. They never happened exactly how he'd wanted them, yet he accepted that they had come true all the same. When Ebi had wished that hot night, he really hadn't meant for his father to be sent away; he'd concentrated on his mother, that was all, and had honestly been shocked when he arrived at Heathrow and she told him that business had taken his father to America for the next year, working on those computers. She told him to draw faith from the knowledge that, had he not been given this most important work, there would be no money for Ebi to come to England. From that point onwards, Ebi was under no illusions. He knew the midwife had been correct.

That night, lying in his new bed in this new city, Ebi projected thoughts of days at school without the presence of Lance. Of being able to walk the school corridors and not find him. Of Lance's friends, perplexed, wondering where he'd gone. Not hurt or injured; just gone.

They kept him off school for the rest of the week while his bruises healed. When the news came, his mother delivered it to him tearfully as he watched afternoon children's television. One of his bullies, Lance, had been playing chicken on the High Street after school. A fast-moving car had hit him, propelling him into the back of a bus, killing the boy instantly. His mother's skin was ashy-grey as she told him, her tears falling to the carpet in a stilted patter, reminding him of the first signs of rainy season. Watching her, Ebi wondered when this particular downpour would fall. He wondered when he would finally tell her the truth.

Two days later, he was back at school. It was difficult for his class to ignore the silent statement of Lance's empty desk, or the pale, drawn faces of Fox and Nathan. The much subdued boys stared from behind the windows of their eyes like veterans of some great war, oblivious of the child who sat across the classroom, brow furrowed, concentrating on Fox with all the might that he possessed.

THE GREAT WHITE HATE

There was a bounce in his step as he walked out of his estate block and onto the city streets. It turned his normal loose-limbed stride into a confident strut of serenity, arms swinging by his sides, eyes scanning everything he saw with the amazed, enquiring gaze of an newly born child. Every object was fresh, exciting, alive with the colours he'd taken for granted the previous day – before she'd let him know. Martin Hill was extremely happy. He could feel the blood rushing through his veins. He wanted to make his joy known to the entire world. He wanted to shout and yell, a far cry from his usual thoughtful demeanour. Martin had learnt to enjoy his own company during his childhood; a seven-year gap separated him and his nearest sibling. He'd grown into a quiet adult. People sometimes mistook his silence for weakness. Maybe now, he'd be treated differently.

Last night he'd finally convinced his girlfriend to stop taking the pill, so they could try for the child he'd wanted since his teens. He didn't know why he was so set on being a father. Maybe it was because he was the youngest in his family and he'd always been well looked after. Maybe when he'd stopped being a baby, he'd looked around and there'd been no one for *him* to care for. The fact was he'd wanted a child of his own for most of his adult life. Playing with his cousins' and his friends' children was nice, but it wasn't enough. He wanted to hear the word *Daddy* and know it was meant for him.

June hadn't been too hot on the idea at first. She was a beautiful girl – lively, sexy, down-to-earth, independent – everything he loved in a woman. The trouble was she was so independent she hated the idea of having kids, and said it would slow down her life.

As a struggling actress (who was surprisingly good), she couldn't allow anything to get in her way. Usually nothing did. But Martin had pleaded and complained and begged, even offering to become a house-husband, if she'd just take nine months out... She'd laughed when he said he'd have the baby for them if he could. That was when she'd relented, and finally agreed. Happily, they'd also thrown their everlasting supply of condoms in the bin.

He was strolling through the Kipling Estate, sipping on a bottle of Snapple, when a cry from a fast moving car reached his ears. He looked up, open-mouthed as it shimmied and stopped a block away. The blood-blotched face of a local Jack-the-Lad leaned out of the window and repeated the words Martin wished he'd imagined.

'Fackin' Nigga! Go back home ya fackin' coon!!! Ya not fackin' wan'ed!'

The car screeched off, the sound of tyres wailing and echoing around the block. Martin felt the good cheer flow out of him with the speed of blood pumping through a major artery. He gripped the Snapple bottle tight in his hand and started to run, full of rage, long legs pumping. At first the driver didn't see him. They'd expected him to just stand and watch, so although they took off with a lot of noise, they'd been more or less cruising their way down the block. Martin had almost caught up with the car, before the man in the passenger seat (the shouter) saw him and alerted the driver. The car lurched forward, picked up speed. There was an intersection at the bottom of the road. Though rage fuelled his headlong run, Martin knew he wasn't going to make it. A roar of anger rose in his throat, as the vehicle took a sudden right. One look at the driver's fearful, excited laughter was enough. He threw his half-filled bottle at the car.

Everything happened in an instant. He saw the bottle smash against the window, and the driver's look of panic as pink lemonade obscured his view. He saw him twist the wheel, too late to avoid his missile. Martin froze. The car disappeared from view with a screech of tyres, the sounds of crunching metal and shattering glass. Then silence.

Shit, they crashed. I made them crash...

His limbs suddenly awakened, he ran.

It was worse than he could've imagined.

From the tyre marks Martin could see what had happened. The car had swerved left, bounced into some parked cars and careered across the road until it hit a metal railing. It had dragged the railing a few yards before hitting a Victorian-style lamppost and come to a violent stop. When he saw the broken glass and wreckage, Martin fought the urge to run in the opposite direction. No one would believe him if he told them what had happened – it'd be a clear case of White v Black. He'd be better off escaping and leaving their lives in the hands of fate.

When he turned to go he found his legs forcing him the other way – towards the wreckage, stepping unwillingly closer. Much as he wanted to run, it wasn't like him not to help people – no matter what they'd done. June always said he was soft as butter. Like it or not, there was no way he could deny his involvement.

As he got closer he steeled himself. People had come out of the terraced houses to see what all the noise was about. He waved them back with a shaking hand and told them to stay away. When he peered through the windows and saw all the blood, it instantly made him feel queasy. There were four people in the car – he hadn't seen the two in the back. One was a young girl who looked no older than sixteen, her face covered in a red mess, her head thrown back, her mouth open wide...

Martin retched. He reached to open the passenger door but found it locked. Without thinking, he pushed his arm through the shattered glass, snaking a hand downwards and pulling at the catch. He pulled his arm back.

'Shit!'

Pain, intense and insistent. Marcus looked at his hand. Glass from one of the windows had torn a chunk of flesh away, leaving a bloody gash. The flow of blood hadn't reached it yet. He cursed his bad luck.

'Don't move them!'

Martin turned to see a middle-aged man standing on the pavement. He pointed at the car's crumpled bonnet.

'I gotta move 'em; that engine's fucked, it might even blow...'

'You've been watching too many movies, young man.'

Martin gave him a hard glare, sighed and looked around at the silent crowd.

'Has anyone phoned an ambulance yet?'

Bingo. There were embarrassed faces.

'I'll go.'

A fat, greying lady with wobbly triple chins moved with surprising speed into her house. Martin turned back to the car and together with a young white guy eased the injured youths from the car. The pain in his palm now yelped for attention. He paid it no mind, even though the dead weight made him want to scream in agony. The male passenger was unconscious, a large purple bump already growing on his forehead. His hair was sticky with blood as though he'd been bathing in it. The driver was fully conscious and although he allowed himself to be pulled from the car, he opened his eyes when he was hefted onto the pavement, glaring at Marcus.

'Git your 'ands off me, ya Black bastard,' he muttered through clenched, yellowed teeth. Martin looked up to see if anyone had heard. His young helper was looking into his eyes, shocked.

Good, he thought. At least *he* heard.

He stepped away from the men and waited for the ambulance.

An hour had passed since the accident. Martin had sat in the waiting room watching people coming and going, in and out. June would be missing him. He felt bad about this, but he had to see this through. Progress was slow – hardly anyone had moved – and the plastic chairs were hard. A Black guy with a makeshift bandage around his head had been there long before Martin, and he still hadn't been seen, even though he'd complained. *Good old NHS*, Martin thought. The only way to get quick service was to arrive at death's door. The four crash victims had been wheeled into curtained cubicles straight away.

He put his head in hands, felt the stickiness and took them away. His hands, shirt and jacket were saturated with large patches of blood. He should've washed but his legs felt weak and he didn't trust them to carry him to the washroom. He kept replaying the moment he'd thrown the bottle, wishing he could go back and change what he'd done.

Swing doors squeaked open. He looked up to see a couple he recognised from the estate. The man was in his forties, short and full of wrinkles, a musty old cap on his balding head. His wife had deep-set eyes, long brown hair and no shape to her large, middle-aged body. Their worried expressions suggested they had to be the parents of at least one of the young men. They spoke to the receptionist, then sat on the plastic seats, no doubt waiting for the doctor to be paged. Martin found his guilt forcing him up, making him cross the space between them, making him stare down into their grief-filled faces.

'Hello?'

They looked up as one, puzzled and annoyed.

'Piss off, will ya? We ain't got no money.'

They looked at him closer, noticing the blood.

'Sorry to disturb you... I jus' wanted to know if it's your son who was involved in the car crash. If it isn't I'll leave you alone...'

'What business is it...' the man started. The woman elbowed his side, looking up at Martin.

'It was our *sons*. What's it gotta do wiv you?'

Martin felt his heart-rate climb, as his bloodstained fingers twisted in and out of one another.

'Well, I have to confess...'

'Confess?' That was the mother.

'... It was my fault your son crashed... In a way... See, they were screaming racist abuse...'

'Your fault!'

The father was up in an instant, pushing a leathery face in his, breath stinking of stale cigarettes. Martin backed away and tried to overpower the man with his voice. The receptionist and other people waiting were looking worried.

'... So I chased 'em and threw a bottle at 'em, and it made 'em crash... I didn't mean fuh that to happen it jus' did... I'm sorry about yuh son...'

'*Sons*, you little fackin' cunt! You Black bastard, dere woz two brothers in dere! Maud, I'll kill 'im, I swear I will!'

The man tried to grab hold of Martin but he was stronger and he easily wrestled himself out of the older man's grip. A hospital security guard stepped in and received a clout in the face from Maud's umbrella. The doctor arrived and was ignored.

'I'm sorry; it was an accident, I didn't mean it...'

'Go back to the jungle, ya coon! They come over 'ere, get fed an' looked after, then they start killin' innocent White kids... Go back to Africa!'

'I was born in Hammersmith,' Martin shouted, his anger igniting again. It was useless. He should've known better.

He looked around, ignoring the staring, shocked faces, then saw there was a clear path to the exit and made for it. In all the confusion he didn't think they'd notice. In a second, he pushed through the main swing doors.

Outside Hammersmith Hospital he slowed down, taking deep breaths of air. Wow. It was a long time since he'd had to listen to that kind of shit and it brought him back to the real world with a bang. English people were usually very smart with their racism. They wouldn't normally shout or scream that you weren't wanted; they were much too subtle for that. They preferred to let you know with a hard look, or by staring like you were some two-headed creature, or moving away like you were a leper when you came down the street. They'd complain that asylum seekers were destroying their country and claim they hadn't a prejudiced bone in their body – in the same breath.

He needed June. He needed to forget about today's incident and start thinking about his future son or daughter. He needed to make love to his woman.

Martin headed home.

In the hospital, the doctor had finally managed to calm the man and woman down, only to find the Black youth had gone missing.

'Ee's done a runner. Black cunt!' the father said. The man with the bandaged head watched with a grim expression of loathing. The doctor asked the receptionist who the missing youth had been. She told him that he had apparently rescued the accident victims. The doctor asked if he'd left a name or address where he could be contacted. She shook her head.

'Ee put 'em there! Ee killed my sons!'

The doctor gave the man a strange look.

99

'Your sons are far from dead, Mr. Fisk. Now if you'd like to follow me...'

The doctor showed them into a small room with easy chairs, flowers and comforting pictures. They sat down, looking nervous and tense. The doctor closed the door behind him, thinking that at least they'd calmed down. The large woman looked up at him, eyes full of tears.

'You said they're far from dead, doctor, but they're *dyin'* ain' they? I've seen *Casualty*, I know what this room means...'

'Shut up woman...' her husband spat.

The doctor surveyed them from behind thick spectacles that made his blue eyes swim like tropical fish.

'Mr. Fisk, Mrs. Fisk. As I said before, your sons are far from dead. Their passengers are far from dead...'

'I didn't know there were passengers...' Mr. Fisk muttered.

'... In fact, all they're suffering from is slight concussion and superficial cuts and bruises. Uhhhh... See the thing is, we need to talk seriously with anyone who's been in physical contact with Aiden since the crash, especially the Black youth...'

There was a hollow silence from the Fisks. They were watching and waiting for the bomb.

'... I'm sorry to have to tell you this, but during our efforts to transfuse blood into Aiden, we found strong indications that he has contracted the HIV virus...'

Mrs. Fisk screamed, her voice echoing into the corridor. She buried her head in her hands and burst into tears. Mr. Fisk sat like a grey stone statue.

Meanwhile, Martin walked homewards, trying to forget about the accident, wanting to wrap his arms around his woman and give her something they could share...

AN AGE OLD PROBLEM

A barren landscape, filled with lumpy little hills, like sand dunes in the desert. The occasional crater, man-made damage in a man-made world. Running alongside were the cracks and fissures of age – long, deep trenches, carved into the landscape by time, branching out and joining others, growing, spreading like a weed.

This was what the boy saw when he opened his eyes and woke up.

He was lying on his back, blinking and attempting to focus on the ceiling a little better. He let his eyes flick up and down, freeing his imagination so he could see an upside-down alien world, lifeless and empty. The box-shaped light-shade destroyed the illusion; there was no way you could work it into an alien planet even if you had the imagination of George Lucas. He yawned, closed his eyes, turned over and pulled his thick quilt around him.

Then he remembered what day it was.

He opened his eyes, rolling them in the direction of his bedside clock. Quarter past twelve. He should've been up by now. He threw off the quilt, stepped onto his carpet clad only in boxer shorts, and peered through his bedroom window. Fog rolled past the houses and trees in thick cotton puffs, creating a world even more mysterious than the one he'd imagined. He slipped on his watch and jeans, struggled sleepily into the first T-shirt he could find, then headed for the bathroom.

Liza was in the living room watching the news, reclining on the sofa. He decided he might as well get it over with. She heard him coming and craned her head around, smiling at him, pulling her dressing gown tighter around her teenage body.

'Happy birthday!'

'Thanks.' He bent down to receive his obligatory peck on the cheek.

'How's it feel to be eighteen?' Liza sipped a steaming cup of tea, eyes shining with envy. His lips twisted.

'I dunno, I still feel the same. I'm glad I can go to the offie without all that hassle from the Pakis though.'

Liza gave him a stern look, but said nothing. He sat on the sofa, putting his feet up on a small wooden coffee table.

'How come you ain' in school?'

She stifled a response, then reached for a small package and envelope on the floor. She picked it up, beaming her I-know-I-can-win-you-over-if-I-try smile. He remembered a school report of hers that had read: *'Liza is polite, intelligent, and more than able to excel in any subject she puts her mind to. She can also be very charming, though she tends to use this as a means to be lazy…'*

Liza had loved that report, showing it to friends and family like it was an A in her GCSE exams. He was sure her teacher hadn't meant it as a compliment.

He took the package and envelope from her, muttered 'Thanks.' The card was another of Liza's dirty joke offerings. He laughed along with the punch line just as he did every year. The present, when he finally got rid of all the Sellotape, was a 14-inch link gleaming from the soft felt interior of its box.

'Damn, where d'you get dis?'

'I can't tell you that, can I? Why, don't you like it?'

'Nah, it's the lick!' he said, taking it out of the box and letting it hang delicately from his hand.

'Twenny-two carat dat is, so don't say I don't treat you good,' she warned. 'Hold on, I'll put it on for you.'

She lifted her arms around his neck and fastened the clip. He looked down at his chest, smiled, then gave his sister a kiss.

'Thanks again, Liza, I like it a lot.'

'That's okay.'

He put his card on the mantelpiece, picked up all the rubbish and headed back towards the bathroom. Just as he crossed into the passage he remembered his question. When he turned, Liza was watching him, as if she hadn't forgotten.

'So why ain' you in school den anyway?'

She turned up her nose and sipped her tea like an elderly lady. 'I'm sick.'

He made a sound in the depths of his throat. 'Sick in the head!'

'Don't laugh, you can ask Mum when she gets back; she said it was all right.'

'Yeah, well, Mum falls for it every time you play sick; I don't. Right about now you look all right to *me*.'

'Well it's a good thing it's not up to *you*.' She stretched out on the sofa. 'Anyway, I don't wanna argue with you on your birthday – I'm here now and that's that. Aren't you glad to have your sister with you, instead of being all alone. Or did you have other plans?'

'Yeah I did. An' I wasn't gonna be by myself. Tyrone's comin' over later. He's bringin' his Playstation.'

'Oh *great!*'

The boy laughed and closed the bathroom door.

As he relaxed in the tub, letting the bubbles soothe and clean his skin, he wondered what his sister was up to. She might've been two years younger, but Liza was smart – probably even smarter than him. The problem was she was wild with it, matured much too fast for her own good. She had the body of a woman and men on street were forever noticing. Liza also had a strange line of reasoning, twisting everyone in her world to her way of thinking, just by laying on that charm. It had certainly worked with his mother. Usually, Liza was off and running with her friend Rasheda not ten minutes after she left the flat for work. That was the way it usually went.

So why was Liza still here? He began to think he knew the answer when he heard his sister yelling.

'Ricky! Your friend's here to see you!'

He hastily patted and rubbed himself dry, slid his clothes on and went to find Tyrone sitting opposite Liza, staring at her with a fiendish look in his eyes. Liza was pretending not to notice, her face turned towards the TV. Ricky slapped palms with Tyrone.

'Happy birthday blud.'

'Safe. You got everythin'?'

'More or less.'

103

Ricky turned to Liza.

'Hey Liza, we're gonna afta switch off the TV. Playstation time.'

'What, now? *Neighbours* is on soon!'

'Watch it in yuh room, you got a telly too!'

Ricky was pointing up the passage.

'Yeah, you got a telly too!' Tyrone grinned.

'Was I talking to you?' Liza snarled. Tyrone, still grinning, put his hands in the air in surrender. 'You got a telly in your room,' she said to Ricky. 'Why don't you play yuh computer games on that?'

Ricky screwed up his face, pointing at the wide screen his mother and father were still paying for. 'C'mon man, how can you compare my TV wiv dat? It's my birthday Sis, can't you jus' 'llow me fuh today?'

'All right, all right…'

She stomped off towards her room, Tyrone's eyes following her all the way.

'You don't hafta leave!' he called, and when she was out of earshot. 'Your sister's buff, man!'

'Shut up, Tyrone. You know dat's outta order.'

Tyrone sighed. Ricky didn't joke where his sister was concerned.

'You got the tings ready?' Tyrone eventually managed.

'Yeah yeah,' Ricky replied. 'He's not gonna know what hit 'im, I'm tellin' you.'

Tyrone grinned. 'I'm gonna buy myself a four ounce chaps, with ice, some sovs… Ay, wha' yuh mum and dad get you for you birt'day?'

Ricky shrugged. 'Nuttin' man. What wiv the TV and all dat, they couldn't really afford it. Dad's bin workin' all the hours God sends, an' at the end ah the day, it all goes on bills.'

Tyrone already had the small Rizlas out and stuck together in an L-shape. Ricky breezed past him, sending the papers flying. 'Mind the skins. Where you goin' man?'

'Jus' gonna 'ave a word wid Liza. Sega's all set up.'

'Cool.'

Down the passage Ricky knocked on his sister's door.

'Who is it?'

'Me.'

'Hold on…' He waited for a moment. The door opened and Liza beckoned him in. 'You banish me to my room, then you come and disturb me! How can I help you now?'

'Jus' by answerin' a simple question.'

Liza sat back down in front of her all-in-one wardrobe and dressing table covered with hair tonic bottles, skin cream bottles, nail varnish bottles and lipsticks.

'Shoot.' She pushed curling tongs into her hair and looked at his reflection in the mirror.

'Well… When I was in the bath I was thinkin'… You're takin' a sickie so you can meet Abraham ain' you?'

Liza fought a losing battle with a thin smile.

'Is that a statement or a question?'

'A bit ah both.'

She continued twisting the tongs.

'Yeah all right, I am…'

He hissed in anger.

'… I really don't see what's bunnin' you. Can't you get it through your head that I'm sixteen now? I'm not a little girl any more.'

'He's nine years older than you, Liza! How d'you mean you can't see what burns me?'

She put the tongs down with a *thunk*. 'Yeah but he doesn't treat me bad, you know, mistreat me or anythin'. He's really quite sweet and very generous.'

'Yeah.' Ricky eyed her open wardrobe full of clothes. 'I'll say dat. But haven't you ever thought he might… You know…'

His sister released her smile.

'What?'

'You know… Want suttin' from you… Y'know…'

'What, you mean like my body?'

She ran a hand along her hips and threw back her head, batting her eyes. Ricky looked away.

'What d'*you* reckon?' he snapped. 'He ain' inta yuh mind or he woulda bought books instead ah garms.'

'Come on, Ricky, we went past that stage *ages* ago…'

Ricky's mouth opened and his chin dropped. Liza's smile broadened.

'Hey, this is 2005 you know.'

'Fine. Whatever you say. I'll see yuh later.'

He left the room before she provided any more detail.

'Hi Ricky, happy birthday, darlin'!'

The girl planted a hard kiss on his surprised lips. Smiling, she brushed past him, leaving him in a cloud of sweet-smelling perfume. Rasheda had arrived. He closed the front door and went in after her.

'Sorry dat's all I got fuh you, I'm bruk, man.'

Rasheda was the perfect partner for his sister, loud and wild (though a brown-eyed angel for her Moroccan parents). She too looked more like twenty-six than sixteen, although you wouldn't have guessed it when she was in school uniform.

Ricky shrugged. 'It's cool, I ain' too bothered. I can cater fuh myself anyway.'

'Oh, 'ello,' Rasheda was saying to Tyrone.

'Raa, wha' you sayin'? Bunkin' off again are we?' he teased, eyes on the TV screen.

'Places to go, people to see…' Rasheda intoned. 'I'll leave you lot to yuh computer. Later.'

'What, you ain' even 'avin' a puff wid us? You girls too good fuh us now or suttin'?'

'*You* said it,' the girl muttered, before she was gone. Ricky flopped down on the sofa, prodding Tyrone's arm.

'Lemme tell you suttin', Tee. You can't chat to Rasheda, or my sister for dat matter, widout being able to drive, pay fuh dinner an' ravin', gi' dem green…'

'… I know man…'

'An' even if yuh do all dat, they'll only *consider* givin' you anythin'. Dat's the women of the millennium in dere. They don't want marriage an' kids, they wanna cheque book n' card.'

Tyrone was nodding. 'Yeah, but what I don't get is – if we're meant to be so equal, why do we always hafta pay fuh tings? Dat ain' equal at all!'

'It's a crazy ting.' Ricky put his hands behind his head and considered. 'Yep, dem lot know what they're on.'

The doorbell rang. Tyrone offered Ricky the spliff.

'C'mon birt'day boy, I'll get dat.'

'Nah man. You know I ain' on it. Besides, I wanna keep my head clear fuh later.'

'Don't be silly, take a couple ah blasts. It's yuh birt'day man!'

Ricky pursed his lips. 'I said no. How many times you want me to say it?'

Tyrone shrugged. 'All right, safe, but I'll get the door anyway.'

'Cheers man.'

Ricky listened to the voices coming from the door. One was deep, male, and instantly recognisable. The man himself.

The tall white man who entered the room with Tyrone had sandy blonde hair, designer-stubble, and wore a wide shouldered leather jacket that reached his thighs. In one hand he held the fascia of the car stereo, in the other a Nokia Orange. Ricky and the man, both unsmiling, regarded one another. The man eventually put his gadgets down and sat on a chair across the room from the boy.

'Ricky.'

'Abraham.'

Tyrone had also turned serious. He sat down next to his friend and lit the tail of his zook.

'How come you boys are still 'ere? I told you, he takes the money at four, on the dot.' Abraham was talking low, glancing towards the passage that led to Liza's room. 'If you mess dis up, you ain' gettin' a second chance. Plenty of people willin' to do dis job.'

'Jus' cool man, we was gettin' ready to leave,' Tyrone said. Abraham eyed the computer and empty packets of munchies on the floor.

'Yeah, it looks like it.' Ignoring Tyrone, Abraham leaned forward, forcing himself into Ricky's line of vision.

'Listen Rick – I know you don't like me. I understand dat…' he paused and sniffed. 'I know you don't like me seein' your sister. I can understand that too. I even understand you sendin' yuh boys to do me over…'

The youths tried to look normal, but couldn't help the way their eyes twitched.

'Yeah, they said it was you two. It's a good thing I know those guys innit?' he laughed. Ricky and Tyrone were silent. 'Anyway, you got the message. I can understand all dat. I jus' think we should let bygones be bygones. Shake hands like adults, get on with business. Which, at the moment, is our four grand. Agreed?'

'Yeah man.'

Abraham stuck a hand out towards Ricky.

'Shake?'

For a split second, Ricky looked as if he wouldn't – then he shrugged, nodded, and shook hands. Abraham turned to Tyrone.

'Shake?'

Tyrone took the hand immediately, though his expression wasn't as welcoming. When they were done, Ricky got up.

'I'll go an' tell Liza yuh here.'

'Thanks. I'll wait,' Abraham replied.

'Clear up dem games for us,' Ricky said to Tyrone, before heading for his sister's room. He rapped on the door.

'Liza, Abraham's here!'

'What, already?'

'Yep! He's waitin' in the livin' room.'

He heard his sister and Rasheda conferring behind the door.

'Come on, I got tings to do!'

'All right. Tell him I ain' ready yet. I'll be out in five minutes.'

'OK.'

Ricky went into his own room. He put on his long winter jacket, burrowing about in a cupboard until he found an old snooker cue sawn off into a thick stump. He swung it a few times, smiled and put it into the torn lining of his jacket. He checked in the mirror. The cue was virtually invisible.

In the front room, Tyrone was sliding the Playstation into his bag.

'Can I leave this 'ere?'

'Yeah man, safe.'

Abraham watched the youths, silent. Tyrone pulled two ban-dannas, one purple, the other red, from his jacket.

'For later,' he said, handing the purple one to Ricky.

'All right, tell Liza we jus' wen' out,' he said to Abraham.

Abraham listened as their footsteps faded and doors were slammed. He studied his watch. When the minute hand had gone around three times, he picked up his mobile and dialled.

'Allo… Police please…' He waited, still shooting glances along the passage. 'Yes… I'd like to report an attempted robbery… No, it's about to happen… Well, I overheard some black kids on a bus…'

He gave them a detailed description of both boys. When he was done, he hung up without leaving his name and sat back in the chair. He looked at his watch. It was nearly three. It took forty-five minutes to get to Wembley.

Rasheda's screeching voice came from Liza's room. 'She's comin' out in a minute, Abraham, she's jus' drying her nails!'

He grinned, leaning over the back of the seat to make sure she heard him.

'Tell her to take her time! We got all the time in the world!'

SOUND OF THE DRUMS

We were walking. Six of us along the empty stretch of dual carriageway, the black tar of the road glistening like snakeskin. Talk was kept to a minimum. The road was carless. The police had blocked it about a mile or so behind us – all five cars of them – though they were powerless to stop the crowds of street youths, travellers and suburb-softened rich kids marching past their pitiful little blockade like some nonviolent army. I wondered if they were pleased with their shabby little display of authority, or if they felt frustrated by their lack of strength. I tell you something for nothing. It was like coming up on E to walk past that barricade with all my fellow ravers. The police had made vain noises about stopping us, but come on man... I mean, how the fuck are eight policemen meant to tell a country of over a million full-on music lovers that they can't party and take drugs until they drop?

It was cold, but our quick trot had peppered our foreheads with sweat, so we didn't really notice the chill. The sky was clear and the moon full. Up ahead there were a few other scattered groups of people eager to reach the location. They were blowing whistles and foghorns. Every now and then we would catch the whiff of whatever drug they were consuming, riding the wind beneath our noses. We'd all sniff and look at each other knowingly. I turned to Filo and thrust out a hand.

'Lemme draw some green nuh.'

Filo had been quietly puffing to himself before I disturbed him, preoccupied with brushing herb ash from his new Nike puffa. He blasted the spliff once more – hard. The snaps and pops reminded me of a forest fire. The head of the spliff sent a reddish-orange light dancing across Filo's face in a way that has stuck in my mind ever since.

'Huh?'

I stepped closer without realising it, relishing the feel of the switchblade in my back pocket, knowing I'd use it if provoked. Fuck, I'd use it even if I *wasn't* provoked.

'You heard me, man. I ain gonna say it twice.'

Filo stopped and held his arms out by his sides before he pointed a finger at me with the hand that was holding the spliff.

'Wha d'I tell you about the way you chat to me, Shivan? Didn't I warn you about dat shit, star?'

He was eyeballing me, offering me out with his body language, knowing he couldn't just come out with it. Bunny put his tall skinny body between us, wild shoulder-length locks swinging, betraying the swiftness of his manoeuvre. While he separated us, the girl pushed her hand into mine, even as my mind grabbed at her name.

Sandra... No, Susan... No...

If I have to be honest, I still can't remember that fuckin girl's name. All I can remember is that she said her parents were Iranian and she lived in Acton.

'What'm to you, man?' Bunny was saying, with a look of real annoyance. 'Why you lot affa argue all the while?'

'Yeah man, why you arguin for, yuh fushin' fools!' the girl's drunken friend slurred, stumbling even as she turned to face us.

I walked away from Bunny and Filo, pulling the girl past her tanked-up friend and on past Cat – a tubby black guy who was ignoring all of us, choosing instead to sit on the curb and build another of his brain-shattering skunk spliffs. I was trying to take my mind off Filo's words, which were replaying in my head. Trying to take my mind away from the fact that he'd disrespected me. Again.

'Ow! You're squashin my fingers, Shivan!'

She pulled them from my clutches and carefully inspected each and every one.

'They're all red now.'

She had a squeaky Minnie Mouse voice that made me squirm. When she realised I didn't give a fuck about her fingers she turned back towards her friend, who was now being helped along the road by Bunny. Filo and Cat were bringing up the rear, no doubt busy smoking that zook Cat had built. I kept walking. The girl struggled to rejoin me.

'How come you lot don't like each other den?'

I ignored her. Pretty soon she gave up annoying me, dropping back to join Bunny and the others, bugging them with her irritating little voice. I was grateful for the solitude of the road, breathing in cold country air. It'd been a long night. It was one in the morning and we were still trying to get there. This was not what I'd envisaged at around nine, when me and Bunny had caught wind of the rave, planning this little excursion.

It was the girl's fault. The fuckin butters girl had made us waste too much time.

The large group ahead of us started whooping and blowing their assorted instruments once more, then started to run. I tried to see where they were going, but the last of them ran off the road into some thick bushes. In the blink of an eye they were gone. I stopped and strained my ears to listen over the sound of my friends talking.

I could hear music. It was faint, tinny and far away – but it was definitely music. And I liked what I heard.

'I can hear music!!!!' I yelled back as loud as I could. They crowded around me, keen to hear too. Bunny was smiling, his grin almost lighting up the dark. I smiled back, eager to please.

'About fuckin time, man,' he grumbled, looking around to make sure everyone was there, trying not to shiver – it was cold and he wasn't wearing a jacket. Confident and fair-minded, Bunny was the natural leader in our little group – a role I knew he often despised. But at times like these his ability to take charge was a reflex that worked like his lungs, or his heart, or the blinking of his large dark eyes. I had a lot of respect for Bunny so the constant fighting that occurred between me and his cousin Filo was a deep and painful thorn in my side. I *tried* to like the brer, but every time I tried, he'd say something else that pissed me off, and we'd only just about keep from coming to blows.

'Fuck dis weather…' Bunny said, raising an eyebrow at me, as I'd warned him to put on a jacket back in London. 'Suh Shivan, yuh sure it's dese bushes dem people….'

A thickset white youth detached himself from his cluster of friends and approached me with a friendly look on his face.

'Any idea were the rave is, mate?' he asked, his Northern accent a surprise to my London ears. I nodded at the thick bushes.

'Dem people ahead of us ducked t'rough dere I think,' I told him. I tried to make my voice jovial. 'You sorted fuh E's mate?'

The Northern bloke gave a knowing smile. Before he could speak one of his friends waved and whistled.

'Oi, wha yuh got, geezer, I might ave summa dat like...'

Bunny gestured to indicate he'd wait a little further on and then he left me to get on with business. Four sales later, me and the Northern bloke came back looking pleased with ourselves.

Without another word we formed an orderly line, following Bunny's towering figure into the bushes. Pretty soon we found a worn trail. It led us upwards. Within seconds we were all panting for breath, cursing the B&Hs and weed spliffs we'd been smoking since our teenage years. The music got louder. Bunny broke through the bushes ahead of us . There were gasps and shouts of exclamation as the others stepped into the field after him.

When it was my turn I looked over the expanse of low-cut grass. The sight was amazing: *thousands* of people (I later learned it was something close to fifty thousand) all dancing and rushing and drinking and talking. Mangy mongrels running and barking between the legs of ravers everywhere. Bonfires blazing. Caravans, tents and vehicles forming a loose ring that covered at least five acres.

And as for the sound system... It was built into the trailer of a large HGV. The organisers had obviously just driven the huge truck onto the field, then peeled back the trailer sides to reveal speakers piled as high as a house. The don't-dare-sit-down beat of jungle spread like a fire across that field sending shivers down my spine. It was all I could do to stop myself barrelling towards the speakers screaming with the sheer delight of it all. For one moment, the sound of the drums was all I heard.

It was time for me to go to work. We quickly began moving towards the large crowd, each of us knowing the others' routine. I told Bunny I was missing and disappeared into the crowd – I still had quite a few pills to sell. People were dancing all around me, huge strobe-lights bathing them with a mystical light. The bassline shook me deep within my torso. I wormed my way into the middle of the jostling crowd, then stood there, taking it all in, before digging out my bag of pills and swallowing my second for the night, grimacing hard at the taste. I was ready for anything now.

It was four am. I was fucked, but still conscious. The fifty thousand were fucked but still conscious. Some mad kind of jungle mixed with ambient was blasting out over the field and they were still raving, still going for it hard, sweating and blowing plumes of steaming breath from overworked bodies. Other people sat by fires, either zoned out or reasoning over large spliffs. I watched all this from where I was sitting – a little hill, some distance from the bulk of the ravers still giving it some in the middle of the field. I motioned to the thick line of coke I'd placed along the centre of a flyer, looking over at the girl lying on the floor next to it.

'Oi – oi, d'yuh want dat or not?'

She struggled into a sitting position.

'Huh?'

She looked terrible. I'd met her dancing with a group of friends near the car they'd driven here and secured our lust with a large wrap of powder. When I left her friends, she'd left too. The girl's red-eyes and smudged make-up, crumpled T-shirt and wild hair were what you noticed about her – what you saw before you realised she could have been pretty and began to imagine her that way. I wasn't really bothered with looks at that time. I was in the middle of an intense rush; the only thing on my mind was relieving the sexual tension heightened by the MDMA and other assorted drugs inside my body. I motioned at the line once again.

'D'yuh want dat?'

She nodded in silence. I gave her a rolled up note and she bent over the flyer, snorting loudly. I watched the crowd move. A pinch of daylight was slowly emerging from the eastern end of the field. Over the west (where we sat) the sky remained dark and full of stars. She sat up, leaving only telltale smidgens of coke dust on the flyer. We looked lustfully into each other's eyes. I leaned over, grabbing the back of her head and forcing our lips together until

I felt the switchblade in my front pocket dig into my leg. Tugging it free, I placed it on the grass in front of us, watching the way she followed it with her drugged-up eyes.

'Wha's dat for?' she slurred.

'Protection, man, don't worry yuhself wi dat…'

We kissed again. I laid her on the grass and turned my attentions to her body, running my hands across her breasts, hips and inner thighs, lingering once I got down between her legs. After long minutes of playing and probing I looked up to see what reaction I was causing.

'*Fuck!*' I cursed aloud, just about resisting the urge to slap the bitch to her senses. She'd fallen asleep on me; she was spark out with her arm over her head at a very unnatural angle. Her legs were still wide open. I gave her a shake. She moaned and stirred a little, but stayed exactly as she was. I cursed again, wiping my sweating forehead with my free hand. I needed some shit *badly*, though even I knew this wouldn't do the hard-on in my jeans any good.

It was time I went looking for the others. I'd seen them around during the course of the night. Filo and Cat had been selling rocks like crazed jewellers. Bunny had been circulating dud E's and hugging every one around him with a loved-up grin. I'd noticed Filo talking closely with the Iranian girl. It niggled me to see him touching her arm, smiling in her face, placing an arm around her shoulder, even though I knew I didn't want her. It was a pride thing. I didn't hang around to watch proceedings because I hated Filo too much to see him near *any* girl I'd talked to – however briefly.

I know it sounds crazy. It sounds crazy to me. Now. But where I come from, the way I'd been brought up, I didn't have a lot to be proud of. So the little things that meant nothing to others meant the world to me. Sometimes those little things were all that kept me going.

Picking up my switchblade, I left the comatose girl and wandered past the remains of the crowd until I bumped into some London guys I knew. I stopped and asked if they'd seen my friends. Frankie, a light-skinned, goateed South London youth, passed me his skunk zook and shrugged.

'I swear I see Filo an' Cat boppin past us a while ago, but dem man could be anywhere by now,' he said in his flat toneless way.

I took a blast of the skunk. My buzz (which had receded to the back of my brain) burst open like a flower catching first light of day.

'Was they wiv couple gyal?' I managed, taking a few more puffs. Frankie nodded.

'Filo was wiv one big-tittie Arabic-lookin suttin,' he offered, grinning and showing off his gold caps. I tried not to let the fact that I was fuming show too much.

'What about Bunny?' I handed back the spliff. Frankie nodded in thanks.

'Yeah blud, I seen my man a minute ago lookin fuh Rizla – he went off over dere…' he pointed to a large cluster of bushes. 'I tell yuh wha though – I think I see Filo an' dat Arabic gully goin dat way too…'

'Yeah…'

I was looking off towards the darkened bushes, thinking how that fucker thought he'd got one over on me. Frankie saw I wasn't really listening, so he left me well alone. The bushes were moving in the wind. Thick leaves were rustling, seeming to call me, while the sound of the drums echoed from behind.

If Filo *was* in those bushes with that girl from the pub, he was a dead man. If Filo was in those bushes, I was going to fuck him up.

Telling the story now, I don't know how I managed to feel this way with all the Es I'd been swallowing. The bushes waved and swayed and beckoned me to come closer. I obeyed, feeling that hard look come over my eyes, the look that told people I wasn't joking around, don't fuck with me, don't even try to talk …

A noise came from behind – it took a second to realise someone was screaming. I spun around to see a hippy-looking guy yelling his head off.

'Shit!! The fuckin pigs!!!' He was emptying all his drugs onto the grass in one quick motion. 'Fuck ya, ya fuckin wankers!!!'

A police van was barrelling across the field a mile a minute, heading straight for the speaker/trailer. I was blinded by head-lights. Then more vans appeared, spreading out on either side until eight TSG's formed a tight V formation. A searchlight lit up the area from high above us, and I heard the sound of helicopter blades. Everywhere I looked, people were running, screaming, dragging along their friends, and dropping large amounts of drugs. Soon, the floor was a carpet of wraps, self-seal bags, Kit Kat wrappers and pills.

I ran for the safety of the bushes. Though I'd done well enough with my Es, I still had three of the fifteen I'd brought out with me – enough to land me back in jail, but there was no way I was throwing them away. Ducking down, I pushed into the greenery, then turned and watched the proceedings out in the field. It was mayhem. I backed further into the bushes as the police methodically chased and arrested dealers and punters alike – some of them people I'd done business with. I saw Frankie and his crew being hauled away, struggling, fighting and cursing. I crept even further into the thick of the leaves.

Around me, quiet – bushes swaying and rustling; in the field, noise, destruction and loud music (which played on despite the raid). The silence in those bushes calmed my mind. Though I felt angry, it wasn't the all-or-nothing red madness that usually overtook me.

In the quiet, I couldn't fail to hear the soft sounds of a woman moaning not too far away. I slowed, stopped; then I saw them – a man and woman on the grass not thirty feet away, the man thrusting deep, his trousers down around his ankles.

I recognised the girl's voice and the Nike jacket – Filo's Nike jacket – bobbing up and down. I squinted. It was hard to tell. Filo had his back to me, so I couldn't see his face and his body completely blocked her from my vision. But the moans… It was her voice, I was sure of it, even though I'd only met her that night.

So I watched. I watched them wriggle and squirm.

At first I didn't register that my breathing had become more laboured. Didn't notice when I freed the knife from my pocket, clutching it in one tight, cold hand. It had nothing to do with the girl. Filo had disrespected me. Had disrespected me. Disrespected *me*.

I was moving before they knew it, before *I* knew it. Clicking the blade open and bringing my arm down again and again –

muting her screams, muting his cries, giving vent only to my will. His arms were flailing, but I crouched over him, my body holding him down so he couldn't move, couldn't turn, couldn't stop the blade from falling. Blood began to fly; somewhere inside me I could hear the girl's hoarse voice go into overdrive. I didn't stop stabbing until the body beneath me stopped moving.

When I told the police what I'd done I cried for the next two days. I still cry every time I think about it. Their sympathies were reserved for others more deserving. I wanted them to know I'd committed a crime spurred on by rage, not by nature. I wanted them to know I'm not really a killer.

I stood over the bleeding corpse, my arm aching, my chest heaving, the girl shuddering and gobbling like a goose, her eyes flinching away from me. I dropped the knife. The girl's breath caught in her throat. I leaned down and flipped the body over, wanting to see Filo's face...

Then the sound of the drums came to a sudden halt. As my hands grasped thick black locks, I already knew...

Bunny's blind face stared up at me, eyes rolling back in his head, exposing pure white, making me yelp. I let go of the jacket – *Filo's jacket*, I kept telling myself. But now it made perfect sense that Bunny might have borrowed it during the night. I knew how cold he had been. Bunny fell bonelessly to the ground as I stumbled. The smack of him hitting the earth started the girl screaming again. I couldn't find the voice to tell her to stop. I looked into the dead eyes of my best friend.

'Bunny man...' I began to sob. His arms seemed to reach out to me, his mouth held open in an expression of outraged shock. 'Ah Bunny, I didn't mean it to be you man – c'mon Bee, get up from the floor...'

But he wouldn't get up. There was nothing more for him to say. It was *all* he could say and he shouted it from every limb, every muscle and every pore.

That's how it was when the police crashed through the bushes and found us there.

ALL CREW

When he heard the beep of the car horn, Barray put on his jacket, making sure the tings were hidden by his Phat Farm T-shirt. Slammed the front door and walked along the garden path. The sky was clear, the air crisp and cool, a few bright stars making a rare appearance. Blinker was arguing with Fiddles over who was going to drive. As usual. Barray and Knots completely ignored them. Kyle would have broken them up, cursing about the Black man arguing over pettiness before casually handing the driver's mantle to Fiddles. Perhaps Blinker and Fiddles were thinking the same, for after a while they stopped, Fiddles making for the right hand side as normal. Barray didn't give a shit who drove.

He jumped in the back with Knots. He knew he should be scared, knew it was strange he didn't feel any emotion. Maybe he just felt numb. He tried to tune out Fiddles' complaints about the driver's seat being too far forward, Blinker's complaints about Fiddles, Knots' urging that they both *Shut the fuck up, dis serious business now*. He concentrated on looking out of the car window as they set off.

'Got some tunes?' Fiddles was roaring. 'We need some badman shit tonight blud. Who's got a CD?'

When no one else found anything, Barray pulled out a clear silver disc. He passed it through the space between the front seats, settling back while Blinker fed the disc into the deck. There was a loud hiss from designer speakers. A second later, jazz was filling the car. The others looked at each other, then at Barray, who had his eyes closed and his spine pressed firmly against the seat.

119

'What the fuck is dis blud?'

'Ask man fuh badman shit an man gi' us Miles Davis to bumba –'

'Thelonious fuckin' Monk…'

'Take it off, man, we might as well lissen radio y'get me…'

Barray's eyes snapped open.

'Fuck you, man; you asked fuh suttin an dat's what you got. I don't see no one else comin' wid nuttin'. You lot don't know 'bout propa music anyway.'

'Here y'are, take yuh rubbish tunes. Ain' even got no beeline blud…'

The CD was passed back. He put it back in his pocket and returned his attention to projecting his memories onto the passing London streets.

8 a.m.

He wasn't sure what had woken him: his clock radio, set to play a grime tape he'd rinsed from Delight FM a few weeks back, or the screams of his youngest sister, Rebecca, only six and liable to terrorist attacks by her brother, Matthew, who was ten – sometimes even by her older sister, Lauren, just turned seventeen. He'd been up until the early hours of the morning, driving around with the dumb fucks who, unfortunately, were his oldest friends, ever alert, constantly stressed, picking fights with people because they couldn't get what they wanted and kicking shit out of them instead. The last thing he needed was a war in his own castle. All he wanted to do was lie in bed until the picture of Kyle on his bedroom door made him feel bad enough to get up.

The kitchen was in a state, as it always was when mum left Lauren in charge of making breakfast. Mrs. Barray had left for her shift as a nurse not long after he finally came home. It was the same four days out of seven; if they were lucky, they saw her for about an hour most evenings. During the day, the kids looked after themselves. Barray, the oldest at nineteen, was given the greatest responsibility and the most headaches if anything went wrong. He argued constantly with his mother over that. They lived in Grove didn't they? Something was *bound* to go wrong.

'Ay Matthew, let go of Becky's hair,' he said, already weary.

'But she punched me...'

'I don't gi' a fuck. Let go. *Now*. Lauren, what the fuck is dis?'

'Alpen, what's it look like?'

Lauren, if he was truthful, was not a nice person. Barray had a sneaking suspicion he had contributed to her evil nature. He tried not to think about how he'd tormented her, joined in with his friends' cusses about her size, and treated her like shit until she got old enough to hold her own. Now she was twice as mean, twice as tough as he'd ever been at her age, a bully who gave hell to all she knew. Here was a prime example. The youngsters were sitting at the table with bowls of cereal and a thin, off-white substance that definitely wasn't milk. Barray noted how Lauren backed away when she saw him coming. He checked her bowl.

'What man, wha' yuh breathin' over my food fuh?'

She was smiling as she said it, knowing she'd been caught.

'D'you kill the last ah the milk den?'

'There was hardly none lef' innit, an'...'

'So what 'ave they got?' His eyes bored into hers. At least she had the presence of mind to *look* shamed.

'I mixed what was lef' wid some water an...'

'Fuckin' hell, Lauren!'

Lauren switched her mournful expression to one of anger. Threatening as she was, Barray had a good three stone and four inches on his sister. The youngsters watched.

'Don't start shoutin' at me, Cujo, I'm gonna call mum at work if you don't leave me alone. I done tell yuh already man! I poured the milk before I realized. What the fuck was I meant to do, pour it back in the carton an' start again?'

'You coulda gi' dem your bowl!'

'There was too much in it...'

There were three knocks and the kitchen door swung halfway open. A head poked around the frame. Ramelle.

'Hey everyone, whassup?'

Grunts and groans from all.

'Hi, Barray.'

'Yeah, wha' you sayin'?'

He was still vex, but he knew his mother hated them arguing in front of other people.

'Safe. Lauren, I got the food.'

'Gi' it to 'em innit. No use tellin' me.'

Ignoring Lauren's usual abruptness, his sister's best friend came into the kitchen. Ramelle was pretty and agreeable, short and round with vanilla fudge skin and eyes like a Manga character. Barray had to hold down a smile when he noticed Matthew checking out her bumper. His brother was growing up way too fast. Unaware, Ramelle got out some plates and put a carrier bag on the table. The smell said everything as Ramelle produced a stack of cartons, opening them to reveal sausages, bacon, scrambled eggs, beans and toast. The youngsters squealed in delight. She loaded the plates and handed them around while Barray avoided Lauren's smug gaze.

'Cheers, Ramelle.'

'Dat's okay...'

She was looking deep into his eyes. His siblings were watching them curiously. Barray took his plate, grabbed some cutlery and headed out.

'Later...'

He went into the living room and switched on the TV. Took a bite of his sausage, then found the bottle of pepper sauce he'd left behind the sofa the night before. Sprinkled some on his plate and tried again. Perfect. It felt good to fill his stomach and watch the TV with half an eye.

There was a light knock at the door. He looked up, still chewing. Rammelle.

'Hi.'

'Hey Rammelle. You not eatin'?'

'Nah, I had mine at home. Jimmy's is messy though.'

'Done know. Wha' gwaan?'

'I jus' wanned to say... Well, I jus' wanned to say I got no hard feelin's about what happened. We can still be friends.'

'Yeah, man, all right.'

'I still like you, Barray.'

'Yeah man. I like you.'

'Okay.'

'All right.'

He went back to his breakfast.

'The other ting I wanned to say is I think you should go easy on yuh sister. She understands what yuh dealin' wid, she does, but yuh can't keep takin' it out on her. It's not fair.'

'All right.'

Rammelle smiled, the movement of a few tiny muscles entirely changing her face.

'You even lissenin'?'

He caught the note in her voice and looked up, smiled back. Studied her for a while.

'You're propa cute yuh know.'

She was blushing.

'Yeah I'm lissenin'.' He looked her dead in the eye. Rammelle's grin held. 'An' I get you, all right?'

'I gotta go college.' Her eyes were cast down at her feet.

'Later.'

She let the door swing closed. He finished his breakfast.

12 p.m.

It took him till then to pluck up the courage to phone his boss, the guilt becoming more acute after a morning of cable chat-shows and random channel hopping.

'Hello… Hello Pete?'

'Barray, what's goin' on? How you feelin' mate?'

'Not too bad, not too bad…'

Apart from the crackles, there was nothing for at least five seconds.

'Any idea when you might be coming back to work mate?'

Good question. Barray pondered it for a moment, picking residues of breakfast from between his teeth.

'Beginnin' ah next week?'

He could almost hear the relief in Pete's voice.

'Barray… That's great news, really it is. Everyone's missin' you

123

like crazy on the shop floor… Denise keeps asking after you, Ronnie's making a welcome back card even as we speak… It really feels different around here without you guys…'

More crackles and distant voices. Barray didn't know what to say. Pete's voice came from the edge of the abyss.

'… Listen, I'm really sorry about what happened, mate. You know you can take more time off if and when you need it, don't you…'

'Sure I know, Pete, don't worry about dat. I miss you guys too. And I'll be back beginnin' ah next week, I promise.'

'Cheers, Barray. You be well, okay? Enjoy the rest of your day.'

'You too mate, speak soon.'

He replaced the handset, thoughts flying like migratory birds with no hope of land on the horizon. It was right what he was doing; he knew that, so why did he feel he was betraying his best friend? Because he'd be going back but Kyle couldn't? It was only work. Without it he'd have to resort to other means of making money, ways that could end up with him locked down. Surely Kyle would have understood? Barray was still on the wing, still far from any conclusions, when he realized Chelsea was standing in the doorway, watching him.

'Wha' gwaan?'

He wrinkled his nose as he twisted his neck to look up at her.

'Nuttin'. Thought you had college.'

'Only got one period today innit? Starts at two, so I thought I'd come an' see my boo in the meantime.'

She came and sat on the couch beside him. As much as he wanted to savour his dark mood, when Chelsea was around he found it hard to maintain. He looked at her lips and recalled how soft they felt when he pressed his against them. Then her body. He'd never been able to resist Chelsea for long.

'How'd you get in anyway?'

'Door was open innit?'

More fuel for the fire. He thumped the sofa, his anger re-ignited.

'Fuckin' Lauren man…'

'Ah leave her alone, you're always on her case. No wonder she smokes an' forgets to lock the door.'

124

'Did you close it?'

'Of course, what d'you think I am?'

They turned towards the TV. It was some daytime soap set in a hospital. One of the doctors was an alcoholic who'd been caught drunk on the job. He was in tears, confessing to a colleague. Chelsea called it his 'big scene'; the bit he'd probably read at the audition that got him the job.

'Should get me on that fuckin' show; I'd smash it, trus' me.'

'Yuh too real fuh dem man... They couldn't cope.'

'You know it... Ay, yuh got green?'

He sighed. 'In my room, in the box.'

'Thanks boo...'

He watched the denim miniskirt sashay out of the room and down the corridor. Five minutes later she was licking a King Size with half an eye on the soap.

'So, yuh goin' back to work den?'

He gave her a long, measured look.

'How long was you listenin' to my conversation?'

'Obviously not long enough. *Are* you?'

'Yeah I suppose,' Barray said, trying to ignore her. 'Pete ain' been pressin' me 'bout comin' back or anythin'... but I tell him nex' week. Tell the truth, he's been real cool about the whole ting, but *booyy*... I dunno man, it would jus' feel propa mad t'yuh know, be on shop floor without Kyle an' stuff. I try an' picture it sometimes an' I can't, yuh know... so I dunno how it can run in reality...'

'It's bin ages though, Jo...'

She was looking at him seriously, smoke trailing from between fleshy lips. They were as juicy as two segments of orange, and he was staring at her again, lost in the contours of her face, her body, her clothes, enticed by the scent she wore, the one he'd bought: Ralph Lauren's *Romance*. When he'd given it to her she'd laughed and said he hadn't a romantic bone in his body. He'd said there was one, and it would tingle like a tiny dinner bell whenever she was around, causing him to salivate like those dogs he'd learnt about in the referral unit.

'I know man... I know, it's tough...'

She put a hand on his.

'You're doin' the right ting, babe. You know you are, so don't worry about it. Life goes on innit?'

'Yep. You got that right.'

They practised smoke rings for a while, then he asked her what she was studying at college. She dug into her Nike satchel and produced a book with a beam of obvious pride. It was a Greek tragedy, Euripides, she said. She was reading the part of Helen. He asked to hear some and lay back on the sofa with his eyes closed, letting her husky voice wash over him. Sometimes, when she got really excited she would throw words at him like Lauren threw punches, and he would try not to smile because he knew she was trying to impress him and he didn't want to put her off. He'd heard her read before; something called *Jitney*, and a few months before that a piece by some British guy, Roy Williams. The dialogue had been bait in places, but he'd liked Chelsea's part; the character reminded him of his sister. This, though... this was new. He'd never heard Chelsea read like this before.

'What d'you think?'

She was looking shy now she was finished.

'Wha' d'yuh mean, what do I think? You was heavy an' you know it Chels... Didn't even sound like yuh come from road an' shit... Where'd you get dat posh accent?'

Chelsea beamed.

'Practice makes perfect innit...'

She was running a hand up his leg now, fumbling with the buttons at his fly and giving him her unblinking stare. As she reached in and took him in one warm, soft hand, Barray leaned over and kissed her, his thunderclouds blown away with the wind.

4 p.m.

They were playing *Grand Theft Auto* in Barray's room when Knots mentioned Parker. He was smoking a fat head while Barray pressed buttons on his controller, moving the computerized car close to the computerized pavement, getting the computerized man out of his computerized car and blowing away the computer-

126

ized pedestrian with one shot. It was rendered so realistically by the 3D graphics, for a moment all they could do was gape. Blood flew in a thin spray on the bullet's impact, began to trickle from the dark hole and then become a fast-running flow. The computerized pedestrian crumpled to the computerized floor. Barray and Knots looked at each other.

'S'how I'm gonna deal wid Dondo when I hol' 'im…' Barray sneered. Knots was killing himself laughing.

'Never mind dat fassy. We should bust dat move on Parker blud, sed way,' Knots choked between laughter and skunk smoke. 'After my man's bin goin' round tellin' everyone 'bout how he's shottin' ki's an' makin' bare dollars…'

They'd been on the Playstation chatting shit and smoking skunk for close on three hours. Directly around them, the room was enveloped in a fine mist that made it look as though it was located at the peak of the world's tallest mountain. Beyond the mist, books, CDs, DVDs, computer games and hoards of other items were scattered everywhere. There was no more than three feet of space between their raised knees and the TV, but four bedroom houses were difficult to come by in Grove, and although Barray often made noise about the size of his room he knew he was lucky not to be sharing.

He'd first met Knots at nursery school and had spent more or less every day with him since. His friend was skinny and over six feet tall. He lived four doors down the street with his elderly parents. Of all his crew, Knots was the man Barray depended on, whom he could trust with his most treasured possessions, could even leave alone with Chelsea and feel cool. Up until a month ago, he would have listed Kyle right up there alongside Knots – he had gone to their nursery school and also lived on his street, six doors down.

'Parker's sellin' ki's?'

'S'what he reckons… He was tellin' Mano bout how he should show man he's got food now, an' when I asked Paris, he was sayin' his cousin's shottin' to Parker, so it must be true.'

Barray was thinking now, his game paused.

'Limo's got good food blud.'

'Done know. Sess too, none ah the punk-ah-doo.'

He sneered at the spliff between Barray's fingers.

'Yeah, mate…' Barray nodded, realizing the significance of such information. 'Suh all we have to do is go down club…'

'Bully my man up…'

'Rob him fuh everyting he's got an' roll out. We need some fuckin' dough right about now. You got tings?'

'Course blud, we in a war ain' we? Fuck you think?'

Knots lifted up his jumper to reveal a dented black handle. Barray got up, dead spliff dangling from his mouth. He went into his wardrobe, moving clothes around until he'd retrieved his gun. There was a box of shells a little further back, which he grabbed and shoved into his pocket. When he turned around, Knots had unpaused his game, his face contorted, the controller dancing in his hands like a ship at sea, the tip of his tongue poking from the corner of his mouth.

'You ready?'

'Yeah, man; jus' getting' some practice in, you know dem ones?' Knots put the controller down. 'Let's splurt.'

It didn't take long to find Parker. People who shot tended to stay close to the ends, where they knew the most people and could guarantee maximum sales. Knots suggested that they go to Parker's house instead of having a street full of witnesses to worry about. The ends was full of people who'd run to the police at the slightest sight of a pistol. Next thing you knew, you'd be fast asleep with armed police kicking off your door and pushing a shotgun into your mother's face.

They walked the five blocks to Parker's hostel and rang the buzzer for ten minutes until some screw-faced mixed-race girl eventually poked her head out of an upstairs window, and told them he wasn't there. They headed for the youth club.

It was early, so there weren't that many youths around. Younger kids dressed in blazers – easy targets for neighbourhood bullies – kept a wide berth from older kids like himself. Barray remembered how older youths used to take his money too, until he got big enough to put a stop to their threats. The easiest way to stop people robbing you was to start robbing yourself. His crew had gained an illustrious reputation in this field, steaming trains both underground and over, even rushing the odd house party armed with semiautomatics. Though it had been tough at their age, Barray felt a sudden pang for the old days as he watched the secondary school kids playing footie with a tennis ball. The days when he hadn't smoked and always did his homework.

Parker was easily recognizable in the Goose Down parka he'd worn every autumn since secondary school, securing his own nickname. He was chatting to a tall, burly white kid they both recognized but neither knew personally. Knots and Barray hung back, watching the transaction. At first, Barray thought the sale was about to be made right in front of them, but Parker and the white kid began to bop away fast, heads down, hands in pockets, past the corner where they were hiding.

They didn't hurry, just keeping them in sight. Pretty soon, they were walking the concrete path that lined the old canal. Here the buildings fell back to reveal a sunless grey sky, the back of a supermarket on the right bank, a cemetery on the left. Colourful barges floated on dark water, tethered to huge metal posts. Before them was the fat Gas Tower. Away from the canal there were so many high-rise blocks and council houses most people never even noticed the tower was there.

Once Barray and Knots got to the concrete path they could easily be seen, but there was only one direction for Parker and the white youth to run. Knots with his long legs soon caught them, bringing his gun down again and again until the white kid fell to the ground holding his head. Barray drew his pistol and sauntered close. Parker's eyes were wide, focused on the side of the white kid's head, where a large red lump was growing just above his temple. He looked as though he was trying to hold onto consciousness, his Adam's apple bouncing like the school kids' tennis ball. Barray grabbed Parker by his locks, pulling his head back as far as he could.

'Open wide fassy…'

He shoved the pistol into Parker's mouth, who dribbled blood and muffled pleas. The youths had well over £2500 between them, which they handed over. Parker also had a Cartier watch Barray was pleased to take, though what he really wanted was the weed. Using the gun as encouragement, Knots made both youths strip to their boxer shorts. They found four ounces pushed into

Parker's jeans. Barray unwrapped a corner of the cling and sniffed. It was Limo's green all right, there was no doubt about it.

'Where's the rest?'

'Wha' d'you mean, Barray, there ain' no rest, man. Dat's all I got lef'...'

Knots pushed the scuffed and battered .32 against the white kid's temple.

'D'yuh want him to fuckin' die today, Parker, d'you want him to fuckin' die right here an' now blud, cos you know I don't fuckin' business...'

Both youths were crying. A barge owner came out to see what all the noise was about. He took one look at the scene and disappeared like a rabbit into its hole. Barray knew they had very little time.

'I think Parker wants to take us to his drum, innit, P?' he drawled, confident that Knots had made his point. Parker nodded, tears dotting his jacket. Knot's lips peeled back, revealing his crooked smile.

8 p.m.

His mother didn't usually get back from work until way past midnight, which meant that evenings at home were lively to say the least. Downstairs in the living room, the TV was blaring Channel U. Rebecca and Matthew were on the sofa with their mouths open, legs dangling and bowls of chicken nuggets covered with spaghetti hoops perched on their laps. Lauren and Ramelle would be in Lauren's room, either chatting on the phone to boys, or smoking dainty little girl spliffs and drinking Alize until they passed out. Barray made sure his own bedroom door was closed tight as he and Knots counted up 4 kilos and 6 ounces in weed, £4000 in cash. Parker hadn't been doing too bad for a small-time dealer with no crew.

'We should do dis more often blud... I ain' seen dis much dough since dem Arabs in Queensway...'

Barray screwed up his face.

'What, an' start a nex' war? I'm tellin' you blud, we're lucky it was Parker. Anyone else woulda come back an' blaze up my drum by now.'

'So you don't reckon Limo'll come den?'

'Over Parker?' He grinned and took a big blast of his zook, feeling the buzz rise. It *was* good green. 'I don't think he'll bother. I mean, would you, knowin' us? Much easier to harass Parker fuh the dough innit?'

'I suppose…'

Someone knocked at the door. Knots and Barray looked at each other and quickly began to put everything away. The door knocked again, three uniform raps. They waited, gave each other another look and nodded.

'What?'

The door opened slowly. It was Rebecca. She didn't enter the room, but stood on the threshold with her head down and a thumb in her mouth. Knots smiled his lopsided, gold-toothed grin. He was an only child and notoriously uncomfortable around kids.

'Yes stush gyal, wha you ah say!'

Barray thumped him and held his arms out wide to his sister, who still remained in the doorway sucking her thumb and blinking.

'Come Becky, come an' sit wiv yuh bruv, yeah? Is dat wha' you want, to come in yeah?'

Hesitantly, Rebecca entered the room and eased herself into Barray's embrace, then eventually onto his lap. He kissed her temple, loving her compact warmth and the baby shampoo smell of her hair. He'd been known to spend hours watching her sleep, marvelling at her tiny features, as if his sister was a little flesh and blood doll made just for him. She folded herself into him, closing her eyes as he picked up his computer controller and pressed the start button. Before the game had even begun, she was expelling little snores against his shoulder. Knots watched with a look that was almost jealous.

After the youngsters had been put to bed and Knots had gone home, Barray was in the kitchen sorting through cartons of ready-made pasta when his mobile rang.

'Yeah, yeah…'

'Wha' blow blud, Fiddles… ?'

'Cool, cool…'

'We see the fassy yuh know…'

'What, Dondo?'

Barray, who had been pacing up and down, stopped dead in the centre of the room, the phone pressed tight against his ear.

'Yeah blud, my cuz jus' belled me innit. She's at one house party in Bush an' she see 'im. Reckons the doorman wouldn't let my man in so he's bin hangin' around outside tryin' to coarse man up an' see if they can rush the door. What, yuh wanna breeze down dem sides?'

'Yeah man. I'm on it blud.'

Barray could feel his heart beat hard. For one moment he wanted to take his words back, but he couldn't.

'I'm jus' gonna see if I can sting a nex' ride, den I'll come an' pick every man up,' Fiddles was saying. 'Gimme 'bout an' hour, yeah?'

'… Nice one blud.'

'Missin'…'

He sat at the kitchen table. The day was here. There was no reason for his palms to feel cold. No reason for them to be lined with a film of sweat that made them shine under the 40-watt bulb. No reason for him to feel so nervous. If they didn't do this thing tonight, people would know that they hadn't and that would make them weak. Then it was only a matter of time before Dondo came looking for them. They had to. He swallowed the lump in his throat, forced himself to get up and bury his head in the fridge, to behave as if it was a normal weekday night when Mum was at work.

Ramelle came into the kitchen, as if from nowhere. She stopped when she saw him, exchanging a look of surprise for one of nonchalance, twisting her hair with a finger, her smile blooming. He attempted to ignore her, turning his back to make another dive into the fridge, but she wouldn't let him get away with that. She stood close beside him. He backed away from the fridge and looked her up and down. She was wearing tight hipster jeans and a small T-shirt that ended just above her diamond-studded navel.

Barray didn't like hipsters on most girls – it usually just made them look flabby – but Ramelle could pull it off. When he'd given her what he felt was justified appraisal, he returned his attentions to the fridge.

'Wha you doin'?'

'Lookin' fuh suttin' to eat. Why?'

'Jus' askin'.'

He surveyed boxed items for microwavability.

'I'm bored,' she said, tired of waiting.

'Issit? Wha's Lauren up to?'

'Sleepin'. So are the youngsters.'

'I know. I put 'em to bed.'

'Well?'

Shielded by the fridge door, he closed his eyes.

'Well what?'

'Well, that means we're the only ones awake, Barray.'

He closed the fridge door, looking up at Ramelle. She had a cheeky grin on her face and her wide eyes were half-closed by the weed. Her hand was resting on her firm, flat stomach, long fingers playing with the piercing at her navel, rubbing the bare flesh beneath. He didn't know if this was a conscious movement or not. He stood to his full height, so that she was looking up at him.

'What's that supposed to mean?'

'You know what that's supposed to mean, Jo… '

'What about Chelsea? I thought you was screwin' 'bout dat?'

'I can deal… Don't worry about me, I can deal. Promise.'

He grabbed her, lifted her chin and kissed her hard, their mouths open, tongues writhing. They ripped off jeans, T-shirts, underwear. He lifted her onto the kitchen table, opened her bare legs and pushed his index finger inside, feeling for the rough spot, knowing he'd found it when she gasped and kneaded her own breasts hard enough to cause them to redden. She grew wetter, his finger glistening. She sat up, reached for him with an urgency he relished and drew him inside. Barray tried to enter as slowly as he could, savouring the heat as he pushed all the way, Rammelle caressing his back, kissing him hard, holding him tighter as he withdrew and eased back inside with more force. She yelped and bit his shoulder, called his name.

When they were spent, they put on their clothes and went to lie on the sofa in front of the TV. They shared a spliff and stroked each other's hair, trying not to think. Barray tried to focus on Rammelle's bumper against his groin, of how the mans would envy his position. He loved Chelsea, he was sure of that, but how could he possibly refuse Rammelle? As much as he tried to justify his actions, he couldn't lose the sensation of having done wrong.

Ramelle was quiet, smoking and watching the TV without saying a word. She seemed different tonight. Something in her manner had changed and it was difficult to grasp exactly what. She was usually all over him, but tonight she was distant. He put this down to her trying to deal with the thought of Chelsea. Halfway through the late night movie that neither was really watching, Rammelle began to shudder. He bent over and kissed her cheek, and wasn't surprised to feel salty wetness against his lips.

Shit…

He leant over Rammelle, her face lit by flashes from the TV screen. 'Ay, I thought you said you could deal…'

'I'm okay…'

'You ain' okay, man. Yuh sittin' here cryin' cos ah suttin' we jus' done…'

Big sigh.

'I ain' cryin' cos ah you, Cujo, so you don't hafta worry innit?'

He frowned in the dark. 'I told you don't call me dat…'

She kissed her teeth and rolled over onto her front, her face buried in the curve of her elbow. She began to shake again.

'Ay… Ay, Rammelle man… Tell me what's up will yuh… C'mon man, don't bawl…'

Between the tears, Rammelle told him about the guy across the block who'd been making comments about her fitness since she'd begun secondary school. One night, he'd followed her home as she cut through the tiny concrete park separating the blocks, pulling a knife on her and raping her on the dirty, cold floor while local residents passed not thirty metres from where they lay. She told the story haltingly, trembling throughout, sometimes violently enough to make the sofa creak. Barray listened. Although he couldn't see anything but the glint of Rammelle's eyes, he could feel her relief when he asked her what door number this guy lived at, what car he drove, exactly what he looked like. When she'd told him everything, Rammelle grabbed Barray's head and kissed him on the lips, snuggling close, pressing her body hard against his. Just before she fell asleep, she told Barray that she loved him. Minutes later, he was watching the rise and fall of her chest, cursing softly just in case she woke up.

12 a.m.

Barray opened his eyes, though he was still projecting his memories onto the passing London streets. Him and Kyle, sitting in the back of some car travelling towards some mission or another, laughing and joking. Kyle stepping between Fiddles and Knots with that funny little smile of his face, as though he was mildly amused but didn't want anyone to know. Funny that. Before the bullets had been pumped into his friend as he stood in line at the *One Nation* Caribbean takeaway, killing him and paralysing two others, Barray had never imagined that he and his bredrins could ever die. Now he knew the truth. This was someone else's story. Life could be given or taken at the slightest whim.

The second call had come not long after Rammelle left. She'd been sober and unable to look him in the eye as she stood by his front door, thanking him for everything, even though he felt he had done nothing but make her life worse. She told him she understood his situation with Chelsea and if he didn't want to sleep with her any more... but, for the record, she cared about him a lot, and Lauren was sick of hearing her talk about him, so maybe it was best if she stayed away for a while. He wanted to say the right thing, or at least to say what she expected, to tell her it was okay, but he was so used to saying whatever came into his mind he just agreed with her, then watched as she walked down the garden path without looking back, her head down and her baseball cap pulled low. A voice in his ear said he'd regret what he'd done. But Kyle was more important than Rammelle; it was as simple as that.

He'd bounded upstairs, gone back into his room for the gun, stuffing it into his jeans, then checked the youngsters as they slept, giving them each a kiss on their foreheads, careful not to wake them. Lauren was flat on her stomach fully-clothed, her weave pushed back far enough to expose her thin hairline. The floor of her room was littered with Rizla and cigarette packets. He threw everything into the bin, even the Alize bottles. After some thought he kissed her too. She stirred and moaned, but remained fast asleep. He closed the door behind him and headed out.

Inside the car, silence fell. They drove through the centre of Grove, past ravers, dealers and the badmen, over the Hill and into the different world of Holland Park. They took a right towards Bush after that and were there in five minutes. Everything in Shepherd's Bush was changing. A plain-looking bus depot stood by the newly refurbished shopping mall. The overhead walkway made up to look like a British Rail 125 train had long been demolished. Even British Rail didn't exist any more. Change was everywhere. Nothing stayed the same.

Fiddles turned off the headlights as they approached the party, and slowed the car to a crawl. Blinker, Knots and Barray drew weapons. The music was so loud they'd heard it half a block away, enticing their senses like pheromones. Nearer, the steady murmur of chatter could be heard and from somewhere a girl was shrieking in either pleasure or pain. There was a group of huddled shadows standing two doors from the actual house, smoking and talking shit loud enough for Barray's crew to hear their peaked laughter just above the tinny treble of sound system speakers. Dondo and his crew. When the car reached the shadows, Barray leaned out of the window, aimed quick and repeatedly pulled the trigger, screaming Kyle's name so the whole world could hear.

COMPLEXION MAKETH NOT THE (BLACK) MAN

All right; now here's the lesson for today...
Queen Latifah

Before we get started – that is to say, before we embark on this journey towards truth and the *reality* of our situation here – I'd like to show the less-informed readers in our midst exactly what I'm talking about with a little tale. Don't worry, I'm not deviating from my *main* topic; which, in case you haven't guessed, is our (the Black race's), absurd preoccupation with skin colour, brought upon us by years of indoctrination by people who enslaved us, took our land, our knowledge and our ancestors, and spread them to the four corners of the earth... *(Whoa! Control – that's what my English Lit lecturer used to tell me – I must control the gateway between my thoughts and my pen...)*

So OK – now you know what this is all about. And I realise it's a touchy subject – a subject that Black people on road don't stop talking about, and a subject that Black people in business suits definitely *won't* talk about. But I've had enough – really, truly, seriously, had enough – and the reason I've had enough will be clear from the story I'm gonna tell after this story – I mean the story after the first story – I mean –

Fuck it, I'll just tell the damn thing and you'll get what I mean, OK?

OK. Here goes.

A dark-skinned Black woman picks up a magazine in her

doctor's waiting room, and proceeds to flick through it. She's not really looking for a change in hairstyle (as her regular stylist had attended to her only a few days before, and up to now the horse hair is still strong and healthy-looking, and her weave is still woven, thank you very much) or a new outfit, or even a new philosophy; she's just whiling away the time, barely glancing at the articles, and quickly skimming through the masses of interviews and reviews.

The more this Black woman flicks through the magazine, the slower her page-turning gets. The further she gets through the magazine, the more she starts to think about the images she's seeing – bold images on bright, colourful, glossy, sun-kissed pages that assault her eyes and insult her pride. She looks at all the straight noses and long hair. She closes her eyes as if to block out the sight of the light-coloured eyes and thin lips. The white woman sitting next to her in the waiting room wonders what's wrong as the Black woman closes her eyes tighter and tighter, thinking to herself: *I do not equal beauty*. No, not really that, because the *man on road think I'm all right*. In fact, it's more like: *they do not think I equal beauty*. And somehow, to that Black girl right there in the doctor's waiting room, in that single moment of self-doubt, *that*, or *they*, are much more important to her. The white woman watches her, concerned, but unable to understand, as the girl lets the magazine fall to the table. Even as the woman peeps at the magazine's cover, and spies the single word – *EBONY* – she still doesn't get it, although she puzzles over what was bothering the girl as she makes her way home on the bus. The girl's desolate face haunts the woman until she gets back to her husband, her family, and her home, where she very quickly forgets the whole thing.

I will not spell out what I intend by that story – you must read and understand it yourself. That is the reality that we, as Black men and women, are living in. I will not attempt to offer a solution to this problem (at the risk of sounding like a smartarse), even though I believe I possess one. And I will not accept the point of view of anyone who uses Naomi Campbell as an argument against my example. For what we want (or what *I* want), in a Black supermodel, is not some blue-eyed, horsehair wearing... *somebody*, who denies her Blackness and working-class roots in order to elevate her ownself, but a true and fair representation of *all* – and I do mean all – aspects of the Black Diaspora. Maybe we don't see anything like this because it differs too greatly from the worldwide view of us as a criminal people – maybe because, like that girl from M People sings – *it's all too beautiful*. You get me?

★

Anyway, the more I prattle on about this complexion thing, the more I realise that you (the reader) must be agreeing with my old English Lit lecturer by now – so I'll get onto tale number two. But first of all I'd just like to say something – *for the benefit of the tape*, as they say in all those crappy American police dramas. Another one they kill in the US of A is – *you can quote me on this* – you know dem ones? Both phrases apply to the following sentence.

I love Black women whatever their complexion.

There – just to get that off my chest. And you, the reader, I know what you're thinking. If you're White, you're probably thinking: *Wha' the fuck's dis guy on? Has he got a complex or what, eh? I tell ya, the guy's got a chip on his shoulder the size o' the Millennium Wheel, mate!* And if you're Black you're thinking: *Wha' the fuck's he even bringin' it up for? If he's bringin' up tings like dat, you better believe you ain' seein' my man wid no Alex Wek complexion gully – blatant!*

But the fact of the matter is, I have to bring it up, and if you saw me you'd realise why. See, I'm what Black people would call a light, red, or even yella-skinned Black man – and what White people would call 'tanned'. And man, the second story has everything to do with my love of Black women (and a little to do with my love of women period – I ain' no racist), because it was exactly that that got me into this situation I'm gonna tell you about right now.

Like I said, I'm a light-skinned, hazel-eyed, Black man. Both my parents were Black, but they were kinda light too. My mum, a lively, beautiful, kindly woman from St. Kitts, always used to say there was a white man in our bloodline. Dad would cough and rattle his copy of *The Sun* and rant about how him *Nah 'ave nuh white man blood in me vein dem...* But even then, even at four years old, I knew the score – I didn't like it very much, but I knew.

I've often found myself in a curious position because of my complexion. At college, the scales would tip at either end: my skin was either completely ignored by other students, or remarked upon in so many different ways I just wished it wasn't an issue. I never found the perfect balance.

The worst thing was the student parties. No matter what kind of girl I went for – no matter how stunning, intelligent, or cute – I always caught somebody looking at me like I was letting someone else down. I always felt a little bad at the end of the night. Not overpoweringly bad, or bad enough not to sleep with my chosen girl, but bad enough to recall the snide glances and curled lips on my first quiet moment alone. Bad enough to recall the hate in the eyes of the hater.

If I left with a dark-skinned Black girl, the White girls wouldn't talk to me because most of the darker girls in my college were into Black power an' shit, an' pro-Black meant anti-White to them. Believe.

If I left with a light-skinned Black girl, the dark-skinned Black girls called me a 'wannabe' and said that light-skinned was the closest I could get to white-skinned – and that – and only that – was the reason for me wanting to roll around on my bed with her for a couple of hours.

And if I left with a *White* girl – Woy! If I left with a White girl –which I only dared do once – man, I wouldn't have a friend who was Black and a girl in that college from the minute we was seen together, no fuckin' joke either...

Seriously though, the one time I did it, I came to college the next Monday an' some girl called Sianna come up to me saying *She saw me leavin' on Saturday*, and, *Don't I have any self respect...* I panicked man, I have to admit I panicked, cause I knew what was comin', an' I could see a whole heap of Black girls earwiggin' not far away. So I jus' said: 'Nah man, she was drunk and she was a frien' so I took her to her yard, dropped her off an' dat's it man! Dat's it!'

Sianna didn't believe me, but I insisted man. Ended up swearing on my mum's life that girl was a friend – an' I know that's cold, but what could I do? The girl was screwing with me when I told her I wouldn't be able to see her any more, an' I kinda regret it cos she weren't that bad... but there were some *fine* sisters in my college, man, with dem kinna back-offs that jus', jus'...

You know what I mean.

I tried to talk to my bredrin Carlos about it, but the fucker just laughed at me, man.

'Don't mek Sianna an' dem gyal twis' you up like so,' he told me, as we got ready to go to the party that fateful night. 'You're a strong, God-fearin', Black back-off worshippin', good lookin' *nigga*!"

'I agree wid you on everythin' but the nigga,' I told him, waiting for him to finish fiddling with the last few buttons on his crisp blue shirt. Carlos was like a woman when it came to dressing. I'd been ready for some time.

'No matter,' my flatmate replied, 'What I'm sayin' is, you can't afford to let dat guilt stop you from havin' a good time wid *whoever you please,* man. You're a man. Live by yuh own code, not no-one else's, man. Shit...'

'OK, OK,' I said, touching his fist, 'I'm gonna do dat, man. I'm gonna start from tonight.'

'I'll be watchin'.'

'Anyone I chose, man,' I muttered, picking up my car keys and going for the door.

By the time we got to the party, my confidence had eroded like limestone. Scores of beautiful girls surrounded us: White, Black, South and East Asian... As I pulled up and parked I could feel the old worry reappearing in my veins. Carlos looked at me and shook his head, guessing why I'd gone so quiet. We got out the car.

Once inside the house, I didn't feel much better. R&B blasted from huge black speakers. Crews of girls hugged the walls, dressed in bright coloured skirts and cleavage-revealing tops. I went to the bar, saying my hellos, and got two cans of Red Stripe.

The two girls behind the bar were stunning. Karen had skin that reminded me slightly of peaches, a blush in her cheeks as warm as the red dusk of a setting sun. Her eyes were bright and chestnut brown, and her lips cast forever in a pout that drove male students crazy.

The other bartender was a girl I'd lusted over for some time. Her skin was blemish-free, as dusky and soft as black silk, and as dark as the night that came after the setting sun. She had curious slanted eyes, long, long eyelashes and a body full of curves I ached to touch. Her name was Zenobia.

We chatted briefly – small talk about college – both were in my English classes – then I took the drinks over to Carlos, who was in heavy conversation with a set of Spanish girls, fuck the looks he was getting. I'd decided I wasn't going to talk to anybody – just have a good time by myself. Carlos introduced me to his friends, and a girl called Rosa – dark-haired, full-lipped and brown-eyed – caught my attention. Within minutes we were talking, laughing and dancing animatedly.

The next time I went over to get the drinks, the atmosphere behind the bar had cooled by a good few degrees.

'Uhh... Can I 'ave two more Red Stripes an' two rum an' Cokes please... An' go easy on the Coke.'

Zenobia cut her eye at me, but it was Karen who spoke first.

'Sellin' it are we, Paulie? After all dem talks you're always givin' about the Black race stickin' together an' all dat, it seems a bit strange to see you chattin' up a English girl.'

'She's Spanish.'

'Pah! They were jus' as bad,' Zenobia said, while pouring out more Wray & Nephew. 'They got us, the Aztecs, an' the American Indians!'

'Who said I was chattin' her up?' I shot back. 'The minute a Black man starts talkin' to a White girl, he gets it from everybody! Black man, White man, Black women, White woman. I believe it stems from the intense preoccupation everybody has with the Black dick.'

They laughed at that. Luckily.

'I'm sorry, but I for one am not preoccupied wid your tings,' Karen said through her laughs. Zenobia just shook her head.

'Go back to yuh friends, man; they're waitin' for yuh,' she ordered, pointing over at Carlos and the others. Sure enough, they were all looking over.

'All right, I'm goin', but she ain' my girl, an' dis conversation ain' over, OK?'

Zenobia gave me a stomach-churning smile. 'OK.'

Carlos stared at me, but no one said anything. The music stepped up a pace, as Hip Hop came on the set.

But I didn't feel right. Every step I took with Rosa was filled with paranoia. She must have noticed, because she started clinging onto me the more I tried to put space between us. Every time I looked around I could see Karen's and Zenobia's silhouettes, watching me fraternise with 'the enemy'. Other girls I knew passed me by, looking me up and down with open disgust. I excused myself from Rosa and went outside for five minutes.

Some African students were smoking weed in the small back garden, so I took some blasts and talked with them about the complexities of the Black woman. Like: they wouldn't give me none themselves, but couldn't stand to see me getting some from a White woman. It just didn't make sense. One of the Africans said that a good-looking brother like myself should have no trouble finding a good looking sister to hook up with. Another said that maybe I wasn't into good-looking sisters as much as I'd claimed. That did it. I went back inside.

When I got back, bashment had come on. Carlos was winin' up with his Spanish girl, and when I looked for Rosa, she was amateurishly doing the same with one of the African students. I watched jealously for a second, and Carlos spotted me, shrugged and mouthed *'Yuh too damn slow.'* I nodded and went back to the bar.

'I see White gyal fin' a nex' Mandingo fe please 'er,' Karen said snidely. I shrugged.

'Minor, man, I wasn't chirpin' her anyway. Gimme a rum an' Coke will yuh?"

'So, rudebwoy, you ah lick de hard stuff now?'

I laughed. 'Jus' gimme the ting man; stop pressurin' me.'

Zenobia came out of a back room with a tray full of meat patties.

'Oh, so yuh back!' she smiled.

'Yeah man, I had to come back an' check on my Afro-Caribbean queens, mek sure dem *all right*, y'get me?'

'We can look after ourselves, thank you,' Zenobia sniffed. 'An' I don' even like the term Afro-Caribbean; I'm Black British...'

'Ah come on, Zenobia, don't go on like dat man... Furthermore, when you gonna come from behind dat counter an' bus' a lickle two-step wid me, eh? You bin goin' on about the race gettin' together too, y'nuh, so help me get it together, man! Come nuh.'

I reached over the counter and took her hands and pulled her towards me. 'Come on, Zen, all work an' no play...'

'Later,' she replied, wrenching her hands away. 'I'll be finished in a hour, den we can dance. All right?'

'I'm settin' my Timex!' I warned. She laughed, a warm, bright, and lovely sound.

'You set it den!'

'I soon come!'

'OK!'

Back in the party area it was slow jam time. Carlos was busy crubbin' with his Spanish girl in a corner – lucky git; it was the same everytime we went out. My former Spanish girl was nowhere in sight. I scanned the room and saw an Asian girl, very pretty, standing against the wall with her friends, a couple of White girls and a Black girl. She'd been staring until I turned her way. She looked down quickly as I stared back, pretending she'd never been looking. I decided to chance it.

'Fancy a dance?' I asked, my hand out, ready to take hers. She blushed and looked down, while her friends smiled and coaxed her goodnaturedly.

'Go on – I ain' gonna bite.'

She took my hand and I lead her onto the dance area. Her hands went around my neck, slowly. I could feel their dampness as they rested against the lump of bone at the top of my spine. She was very, very pretty. I whispered my name to her. She smiled and said her name was Mimi. Slowly, we started to move together.

We danced for around three or four songs. Her body felt good – small, snug and warm – against mine. Her parents were from Thailand, but she'd been brought up in Tottenham for most of her life. She was studying occupational therapy, and said she was really enjoying the work, though she thought it would be even better when she got a placement. I told her about my course in journalism, and my hopes that, one day, I could work for a decent, broadsheet Black paper. She said she understood; there were no

papers for British born Thai people either; she understood the
way it felt to be ignored. It was only three or four songs, but that
was the closest I'd ever felt to a complete stranger in my entire life.

I went back to bar to get more drinks. Zenobia's icy glare was
back.

'I see you couldn't wait,' she muttered between her even white
teeth. I sighed.

'What am I supposed to do, wait aroun' for you to finish, an'
not dance wid no one? It's a party man, I'm supposed to be havin'
fun. You're supposed to be havin' fun!'

'So how come I ain' seen you havin' fun wid no Black women,
eh? Is it because for all your big talk you ain' no different from
Frank, or Chris, or Mr. Bloody Motivator...'

She broke off and stared at something. I looked around. Mimi
had come to the bar.

'Is anythin' up?' she asked. I shook my head, feeling embarrassed. Zenobia's eyes rested on me like the eyes of a judge about
to cast sentence on a convicted murderer.

'You haven't got my drink yet,' Mimi gave a nervous laugh,
looking from my face, to Zen's, to Karen's, who was hovering
nearby, eavesdropping on every word. 'I wanned a brandy an'
ice...'

She stopped when she realised I was staring somewhere else.
Anywhere where I couldn't see her. I mean, I couldn't look at her,
I felt that bad. I felt small, tiny – in fact I felt like the world's
smallest hypocrite. Mimi looked over at Karen's and Zenobia's
resolute faces – and she knew who they were all right. Both girls
were well known for their militant attitude where the Black race
was concerned. Then she turned to me and said, 'OK, Paul... OK.'

And she walked out of the party.

I went back outside after that, my mind a maze of conflicting
thoughts and feelings. Was I right? Was I wrong? Even up to now,
as I write this down, I can't work out whether I did the right thing.
Something tells me I'll never know.

Nothing really happened after that, beside this one thing with
Zenobia. I went back inside to find the party was winding down.
Carlos had no doubt left with his senorita, for there was no sign
of him. I went back to the bar feeling like shit, and thought that

since I'd thrown away the chance of a night with an Asian Princess, I might as well throw caution to the wind and try my luck with a Black Queen. I stepped to the bar with a confidence born out of having no regard for the consequences and found the girls tidying up. I called her name.

'Whassup?'

'I wanna chat, Zen.'

'I'm busy now, Paul.'

'Two seconds, man, c'mon two secs.'

She looked up and must have seen the desperation on my face.

'OK ... OK ...'

She crossed the counter and stared at me with her hands on her hips.

'Lissen Zen,' I began, 'it's crazy, man; you know dis whole thing dat happened tonight is...'

'It's cool, Paulie. If you don' like Black girls dat's your business. Plenty of Black men dat do.'

She went to turn away but I held onto her arm and pulled her gently back.

'Lemme finish, man. I... lissen, I do like Black girls, Zenobia, believe me I do. I mean... I like women, beautiful women, dat's what I like. I like *you,* Zenobia.'

She covered her mouth with her hand and stifled an abrupt giggle, but I heard it. I fuckin' heard it.

'I'm sorry, Paulie,' she said quickly. 'I know I sound rude, but I thought you knew...'

'Knew what?'

'Dat I don't go out wid mixed-race guys, dat's what...'

'Huh?'

I was honestly shocked.

'I don't go out wid mixed-ra...'

'Yeah, yeah, I heard you...' I stood still for a second, taking this in. 'But I ain' mixed-race, Zenobia. An' in dat Black awareness meetin' las' week wasn't you sayin' we're all Black no matter...'

'I did, but dat has no bearin' on my sexual preference,' she told me. 'You seem jus' as confused as Karen. So even though you ain' mixed-race, you seem to've bin landed wid the same burden. *Know* what you want. *Dat's* why I don't see mixed-race guys, or

146

for dat matter, light-skinned guys. Lissen, I'll see you on Monday, OK? See yuh aroun'.'

She went back to bar. I left the party and drove home. I couldn't sleep for a long time. And that was that.

★

I saw Mimi not long after that. It was in college and I was between lessons, crossing the building. She looked fine man – she was wearing those figure-hugging jeans and a baggy woollen jumper that made her look small and kind of defenceless. I called over to her, and she looked over, saw me and smiled – then remembered. She put her head down and walked away as fast as she could. I was gonna follow an' explain, but then I got to thinking I didn't really blame her. Do you?

SMILE MANNEQUIN, SMILE

The skin was almost perfect and yet cold. A sunset glow of rusting tan spread across the lithe body. Hints of red dotted in amongst brown. A scattering of freckles running from right shoulder to elbow. A blemish-free face, even in tone. Adams tended the skin, rubbing oils deep into the surface, making it shine with an appearance of good health. There were very few defects, something that amazed her. That she, such an imperfect creature, could create something so close to perfection, so unreal.

The morning Mr. Yoshimoto came, Adams was almost finished and feeling pretty pleased with herself. Despite the near perfect result, this one had been difficult; she hadn't made the armature quite right and her casts of the feet had gone wrong too. She'd had to remould the latter, though when she looked at the mannequin now she knew that only an expert would see the inaccuracies. She blamed her mistakes on the daydreams that had consumed her while she worked, as well as the bottle of red wine she'd downed. The wine coalesced with her memories, thinking about the time she broke a molar on barbecued ribs. She was drunk. They were all drunk. It had been her wedding day.

The first she knew of Mr. Yoshimoto was the realization that someone was ringing her workshop buzzer. She left her work and watched him lurk uncomfortably at the bottom right corner of the black and white monitor. He was short and nondescript, wearing a suit, tie and matching hat; some dark colour she guessed. He looked Asian, though she wasn't sure. He spoke her name slowly and seriously into the tiny microphone, asking if it was possible to spare him five minutes. He'd made no appointment. Adams buzzed the man in and waited.

Yoshimoto entered the workshop seconds later, looking up, down and around at the forest of body parts, mouth wide open. Then he saw Adams. He immediately bowed with deep a tilt of the head. Unconsciously, she did the same. When they looked up, she could see that his face was large for such a small man, almost perfectly round.

'Good afternoon.'

'Domo origato.'

The man beamed, displaying a jumble of misplaced teeth and pink gums.

'You speak Japanese?'

She smiled in return. 'No, just visited Tokyo for a month. Picked up the basics, that's all.'

'But you try. That is very good.'

Her head was still nodding like one of those puppies in the rear window of a car. She forced herself to stop.

'Thank you. Now, what can I do for you, Mr....?'

'Yoshimoto. Konishi Yoshimoto.'

Adams shot him a look tinged with disbelief – tempered slightly, in case she appeared rude.

'What, you mean like the writer? Banana Yoshimoto?'

'Yes, yes; you know her too?'

Adams guided Yoshimoto towards her office space, a small cubicle with a computer and phone in a corner of the workshop. She drew up a chair and eased him into it while he continued to beam. She wondered if the knowledge that she'd been to Japan made him so cheerful, or whether he was always that way.

'I do, Mr. Yoshimoto. So, you begin by telling me how can I help and I'll make the tea. Is that a deal?'

'I accept.'

She flipped a switch on the kettle and retrieved some battered mugs and tea bags from a cupboard. When she'd made the tea, Yoshimoto was holding a magazine open on his lap. The pages were all full colour, glossy and brightly presented. Adams used the pretext of putting a mug down beside him to peek at the magazine, but she couldn't quite see what it contained. Yoshimoto was concentrating on the pictures before him with an almost religious reverence.

'I want you to make a doll for me. Like the ones in this magazine.'

She frowned.

'You did check out my website before you came here, right? You know I only take mass orders from retailers?'

'Yes, I read that. But my need will be equally matched by my money, Miss Adams… I am prepared to pay £5000 for your services…'

She tried to retain her casual demeanour, but she could feel surprise light up her face. Before she knew it her arm was outstretched, fingers beckoning.

'Can I see that a minute?'

'Of course.'

She took the magazine from him and opened it. For a long time after that she was too stunned for speech – the only sound in the workshop was the rustle of glossy paper as she turned pages. What she'd thought was a magazine was in fact a brochure, seemingly produced to promote the sale of life-sized Japanese dolls. They were fully-clothed and placed in a number of 'real-life' poses – sitting by a window, lying on a bed, one even perched on the toilet – still fully clothed. It was difficult for Adams not to feel admiration alongside a vague disquiet. Even in a summer dress or a blouse and jeans, the dolls still seemed overtly sexual in their intent. They were cast with breasts, pretty young faces and even what one line of advertising referred to as a 'marriage-hole'. Yet it was the artistry of the unknown mannequin-maker's work that really stirred her interest. The faces were so pretty, so lifelike. Adams wondered how hard it would be to recreate that type of subtle, understated beauty. All the mannequins she'd ever designed had been so obviously false she'd never even considered making them pretty. But there was the issue of earning £5000 for something that would cost peanuts to make.

She raised her head from the brochure. Yoshimoto was watching her with a concentration that was a little disturbing, no longer quite so cheerful. She noted that he hadn't said a single word or drunk from his teacup since he'd passed her the brochure.

'Can I keep this?'

She waved the limp booklet.

'Of course.'

'And I'll need half the payment up front.'

Yoshimoto immediately began digging into his inside jacket pocket. He produced a chequebook, a gold pen and a small, slim-line silver case. He opened the case and gave Adams the embossed business card with a flourish.

'Call this number when you have finished. It will take how long?'

'I'd give it six weeks or so. If it's gonna take any longer I'll let you know.'

'Finish within six and you get an extra thousand bonus.'

Interesting. She studied the card he'd given her; the title, Konishiwa Enterprises, told her nothing about the business her new client was involved in, but that was okay. She figured the less she knew about a man who wanted to buy a life-sized doll complete with 'marriage-hole' for twice the rate advertised in his glossy little brochure, the easier her job would be. The phone number was local, she recognised that. By the time Adams had read the card and placed it in her little desk drawer, Yoshimoto was holding a company cheque for £2500 by one corner, beaming again.

'You will do a good job, Ms. Adams. I have made a great deal of enquiries about this matter. Everyone tells me you are the best. You are even named after a famous doll, isn't that correct?'

Adams blushed, busying herself taking the cheque and putting it in her small desk safe, avoiding his eyes.

'Yes; my full name's Barbara, but I use Barbie for business' sake really… It's been my nickname ever since I got into manne-quins…'

He was watching her with a relaxed look in his eyes again. She passed him her own business card just to give her hands something to do.

'I have embarrassed you. I will leave now and let you continue your work.'

Yoshimoto got to his feet. She saw him to the workshop door, her mind racing with questions she dared not ask.

'Thank you, Mr. Yoshimoto. I'll call in a week, let you know how it's going. Okay?'

'I would appreciate that very much.'

He bowed so low she could see his thinning crown. Adams did the same, smiling.

'Good afternoon, Miss Adams.'

'Good afternoon…'

She was laughing in quiet disbelief before the workshop door had closed behind him.

At first, Adams considered using herself as a model for the body armature; she was slim and around 5' 7", which she guessed matched the models in the brochure; and it would save her a few hundred pounds. One long look in the mirror changed her mind. There was no hiding her African figure, even if it came via Antigua. She would have to take the search outside her workshop. In the great TV game show tradition, she phoned a friend, who advised that Adams try the School of Oriental and African Studies down in Russell Square. Within four days she'd posted an ad on the college notice board and received six pictures from likely candidates. She was immediately sure which one she wanted. Sayaka was a talkative, giggly student from Kyoto. She was taking African Politics, which Adams found highly curious, and had lived in Kenya, Zambia and Ghana before she'd come to England. Sayaka was the perfect model: cool and detached, able to sit still and not fidget… She was beautiful too; her skin glowed a creamy butter colour and her lips pouted like a tiny pink flower, the upper petal slightly larger than the lower. Adams took Polaroids, noting the black beauty spot just above her upper lip. She faxed the photo to Yoshimoto for his approval, which was rapidly given. The women agreed on a price, £300 for the whole sitting, and decided to begin work the very next morning.

Over the next four days, Sayaka attended the workshop every afternoon for three hours at a time, stripping down to her knickers and letting Adams wrap her in bandages like an ancient Egyptian, and then pour fine casting plaster over her limbs, torso and eventually her whole head. She was patient and compliant as Adams had judged, blasé about shedding her clothes, which made the whole process so much easier. Adams turned up the heating and kept her eyes on the work. Sayaka's body was shapely in a way she'd never seen before: thin arms, a generous torso, firm yet small breasts, a minuscule waist leading to widened hips, the faintest raindrop curve of a bottom. She giggled a little when Adams applied the plaster down there, but other than that, Sayaka never made a sound. She held herself perfectly still, chest rising and falling imperceptibly, serene features raised to the lights. Adams wondered if the Asian girl could hear her attempts to regulate her own breathing, or whether it sounded as loud as it felt.

Soon, her model was completely cast. After the last session, Adams took Sayaka into her little office cubicle and paid her the £300 in cash. It was an awkward moment, both women aware that their reason for meeting had dissipated like sugar in the tea Adams made every day. Until that point, they had almost believed they had become friends. They swapped numbers and agreed to stay in contact, though neither intended to. Sayaka waved a dainty little hand and left the workshop, her pretty blue and yellow summer dress dancing as she walked. Adams never saw her again.

She waited for the plaster to set, flicked through the brochure, took a look on the internet for the company website. The daylight in the workshop dimmed and silhouettes of severed limbs made dark shadows on the bare walls. It would be a tough job, one that she hoped she could do justice. Yes, the dolls were slightly strange to look at, and the thought of their use was disturbing, but she couldn't help noticing how close they were to the real thing. Her time in Japan had been limited – four weeks teaching art to primary school children in Tokyo. Though she'd partied and got stoned and generally hung out with a few Japanese, she'd never seen any women as up close and personal as Sayaka. She'd always thought Asian women beautiful, especially the Japanese. Now, she realised how flawless the real thing could actually be.

In order to finish by Yoshimoto's deadline, Adams decided to work nights and sleep amongst the disembodied limbs, heads and torsos – which wasn't unusual. Fuelling herself with more tea, she used copper pipes, mechanic's hose clamps and a bench-mounted vice to create a skeletal torso based on Sayaka's dimensions – a laborious and sweaty task. Still, she'd always found the bending and tugging therapeutic – a chance to think and maybe even realign her chakras. She turned on the radio for company's sake, but found the presenter's voice drowned out by her own inner voice, her own memories. They never left her head. They were buried deep in her brain, waiting for moments like these to scratch their way to the surface, bawling for attention, leapfrogging from one to another: from her hen night, to her broken molar, to her wedding night (a stoned disaster) and subsequent honeymoon (Butlins). Indeed, the only time Adams ever thought about Frank, her estranged husband, was when she was hard at work. He had been a weak, unruly man, addicted to drugs more than her, whereas she'd used them as a temporary escape, nothing more. They were together three years before the penny finally dropped: he wasn't going to change, even if she did. She was twenty-four years old with a chance to start again. The day she finally left the squat, Adams had been plagued by the thought that she'd never see him again. Now she knew that what she'd feared had in fact been hope.

She lived on the hard wooden floors of friends and acquaintances for months after that until she was accepted into St. Martin's Art College the following year. She was given her own room along with a shared bathroom and kitchen within the halls, the first space she'd ever had the chance to call her own. Surrounded by students of all ages and nationalities, Adams kept pretty much to herself, reading, cooking and attending the odd art exhibition if her studies and funds permitted. Amongst her fellow students were some Japanese, who formed a tight group, like fingers curling into a fist, whenever they came into class. Adam's curiosity was raised by their cheery manner, their quiet politeness and easy beauty. She began to hang out with them, though she never really got close to any of them. When she graduated she kept in contact with one, a quietly crazy and talented twenty-one-year old named Junko. That was how she learned of the teaching job in Minowa. When she returned home Adams knew that she'd rather practice art than teach it. She applied for the first job that came her way, an apprenticeship at a mannequin workshop in West London.

There, her life was shunted onto a new, though not an entirely unfamiliar track. Adams' mentor, Barry Megson, was a cold, clinical man who rarely had time for jokes or even smiles – which

154

suited her just fine. He taught her everything she knew, there was no doubt about that, but apart from the lessons in plasterwork they rarely spoke. She fell deeply in love, first with Megson, then with the art of mannequin-making. They slept together once and decided never to do it again. Megson claimed he loved his wife and didn't want to complicate things. Adams, wanting to hold on to her job more than her fleeting love affair, let him go without a fight. When Megson died a year later from a sudden asthma attack, Adams was both shocked and grateful to find that he'd left her the workshop in his will. His widow tried to contest it, but there was nothing she could do. Adams ignored her phone calls and threatening letters until they trickled to a slow halt, throwing herself into her work. The only friendships she formed after that were work-related, as were her pleasures.

Once the armature was finished, Adams wrapped it in chicken wire and carried the skeleton into a small back room behind the main workshop, sitting it up against a large plastic bin filled with soaking clay. She spent a couple of hours spreading an even layer of gloopy substance all over the chicken wire until it was completely covered. This would anchor the weight of the sculpture to its copper skeleton. Next step was to cast the doll using Sayaka's body mould. That took three bags of Herculite no.2 plaster, with some left over for the feet, hands, arms and legs. The hands and feet were made using Alginate casts of another model, a lanky Australian teenager she'd met in the tea section of a Turkish supermarket in Harlesden. The girl, Alex, had the most surreal, elongated fingers and toes Adams had ever seen. They looked almost alien in real life, but were beautiful and elegant when cast in Herculite. She didn't normally use the same model for hands as well as feet, but since she'd found Alex there'd been no need to look elsewhere. She had to wait for Sayaka's body parts to dry, which took another day, and then attach metal fittings for the wrists, waist, shoulders, and neck. This allowed her to add movable limbs and a head.

By the beginning of the fifth week, when she'd completed the sanding, Adams was forced to smile at her handywork. The doll looked undeniably sexy. Placed beside her previous mannequins, the difference was amazing. Forcing away her pride, not allowing the thought to grow roots, she tentatively spread some extra plaster on the mannequin's rear to make it more pert. While she waited for Sayaka to dry she began to read. It seemed fitting that she'd chosen Murakami; she'd ordered *Sputnik Sweetheart* over the internet years ago but had never opened it. The concise, simple poetry of his prose brought back pleasant memories of Minowa; the story of Sumire's infatuation with Miu drew her in easily, like dipping a toe in warm bath water. She dug out some traditional Japanese CDs bought during her month there, and drank green tea from the local corner shop. When the torso was dry she went back to work, getting out her brushes and paints, mixing a deep yellow colour that almost bordered brown. Of course, the paints had to be modified to fit the original colour of the mannequin, but she achieved the effect she wanted. Adams painted well into the night before falling asleep on an old sofa. The next day, she continued her task.

When everything was finished, including make-up of pale pink lipstick and dark black eyeliner, Adams opened a box that contained yet another internet purchase – a shiny, almost blue/black, shoulder-length wig. She had searched long and hard for Asian hair, and was referred to a small company near Carshalton by her regular Wandsworth supplier. Slowly, breathing lightly, Adams walked over to the mannequin, which had taken centre stage on the workshop floor, away from the other mannequins. Gently as she could, she placed the wig on the bald head and at once burst into an involuntary giggle, one hand lightly touching her lips. She stepped back, a broad smile flooding her face.

'Hello Sayaka,' Adams breathed, unaware that her mouth had even moved, let alone that she had spoken. Yet she had voiced the truth. The doll was now the spitting image of the Japanese student. The closest to a human being Adams had ever created – and here Adams balked at the thought – as lifelike as a work by the late Duane Hanson. It was the attention to detail, the little imperfections all human beings possessed, that made her new creation so perfect.

She rang Yoshimoto the next morning after spending another night sleeping in the workshop. He didn't seem at all put out at the prospect of shelling out an extra thousand pounds, sounding as cheerful and lively as she'd expected. He told her he would arrive at her workshop by early afternoon, one p.m. at the latest. Adams nodded and put down the phone without saying any more, feeling a little tired, a mite pensive. She'd been unable to stop herself waking during the previous night and standing before her mannequin, unable to stop herself from shaking her head in pride. It was truly difficult to believe that Sayaka had come from her own hand. The doll was her best work ever, real enough to have been born of the womb. She'd run her fingers up and down the cold arm, along the line between her breasts, even fingered the hard depth of her marriage hole – putting this last intrusion down to morbid curiosity. She regretted the hole as soon as she'd finished drilling and couldn't imagine why anyone would want to violate beauty in such a manner. Nevertheless, it was done now, and done to Yoshimoto's specifications. How she felt about such things was irrelevant.

He rang the workshop bell at five to one. It was raining and he came inside with tiny droplets sprinkled on his head and shoulders like dandruff. He seemed agitated or somewhat hurried, bowing quickly and shedding his black Inspector Clouseau raincoat before she could even complete her Japanese greeting. His actions caused her to frown; she couldn't stop herself, and Yoshimoto couldn't help but notice. He explained that he was feeling sick and requested the use of Adam's lavatory. She ushered him halfway there, both of them pointedly ignoring the object that stood in the centre of the workshop floor, draped in a sky-blue dustsheet from head to toe. Walking back into the workshop, Adams heard the lock click and the toilet seat clatter. She looked at the concealed mannequin once more as she crossed the room towards Yoshimoto's raincoat. She had very little time.

She knew that what she was about to do was crazy. The thought had only occurred when Yoshimoto walked through the door. The problem had been the how – until he took off his raincoat and rushed to her toilet. Such divine providence came along only once in a while. Adams reached into his jacket pocket and there they were – Yoshimoto's keys complete with a blue BMW tag. Moving fast, her ears straining for sounds of the businessman's progress, she grabbed the first piece of clay she could find, flattened it with one hand, and then pushed each key into the soft lump, one after the other. Three perfect impressions were left, lined up like fossils: a house key, a Yale and his car key. Quickly, she trotted to her battered sink and washed the clay off before drying the keys and putting them back into his raincoat, being careful to return the bunch to the exact pocket she'd found them in. She hid the clay in a desk drawer and then sat on the first available chair, crossed her legs and picked up a trade magazine. Yoshimoto came back five minutes later looking pale.

'Are you OK?' she asked, honestly worried by his pallor.

'Something I ate disagreed with me,' he admitted, looking forlorn. 'These bloody business brunches will be the death of me.'

'Would you like a glass of water? I have Alka Seltzer too.'

'Yes, yes, you're very kind. That would be marvellous.'

'I'll just show you your mannequin, then I'll fix it right away,' she said, walking over to the dustsheet and unveiling Sayaka. She was watching him the whole time. Even if she hadn't, Adams would still have heard Yoshimoto's sharp intake of breath when he laid eyes on her creation, and the long exhalation that followed, like the slow release after orgasm, impossible to stem or control. Ignoring the involuntary shudder that ran through her, she smiled and said, 'I'll get your water,' but she could tell he wasn't hearing her. He was staring at the counterfeit Sayaka as if nothing else in the room was there, as if nothing else in life mattered. It was then and only then that she was secure in the knowledge that she could not let perfection go. After all, it was her creation, made with her own hands. Sayaka belonged to her.

She made the Alka Seltzer and brought it to Yoshimoto, who drank it down in one go. Still holding the glass, still staring at Sayaka, he seemed unable to grasp words. He stepped forwards, touched her face and hair. Adams looked at the floor.

'Is she what you wanted?' she asked, when her heartbeat slowed to an acceptable pace.

'More,' Yoshimoto replied, and she could feel his sincerity. 'Have you named her?'

'Sayaka.'

'Perfect,' he breathed. The word was hardly audible.

'Yes,' Adams said, still looking at the dusty floor. 'That's what I thought.'

They replaced the dustsheet and carried Sayaka to the BMW, Yoshimoto taking the head and Adams the feet. He opened the boot, placed the doll inside, shut it with a satisfied smile. Adams tried to match it but couldn't muster enough feeling, even when he gave her a cheque for the remaining £3500. Her gaze kept inching towards the car like ball bearings attracted to a magnet in their midst.

'You are a genius,' Yoshimoto told her. 'I have many friends who would enjoy your work. Can they call you?'

'Of course,' she said, though the weight of each word bowed her head as though there was a giant hand on the back of her neck, pushing down. Yoshimoto stood before her, stiff and formal.

'It has been an honour to meet you.'

'An honour to meet you too, sir.'

He was gone before she knew it, the BMW easing out of the industrial estate, leaving her with an ache she hadn't felt since she was a teenager.

She had a local locksmith for a friend who'd long fancied her from afar. The keys were cut within the hour. All she had to do then was head for the address on Yoshimoto's business card, another industrial estate just off Scrubbs Lane. She took the train to White City, reading *Sputnik Sweetheart*, and walked the rest of the way, sharpened splinters from the newly cut keys digging into her thighs. She was fully aware that what she was doing was irrational, illegal and very stupid. She should wait, think this thing out before going off on such a sudden whim; but she could not. Only very rarely did Adams get an urge as strong as this. Indeed, it wasn't so much an urge as some long-buried, primal instinct that emerged just like her memories. Like when she'd left Frank. One day she'd woken up to a morning no different from any other and known it was time to go. Didn't need to pack any bags because she had nothing to take. Simply got out of bed, left him sleeping on his stomach, dead to the world, opened the front door and walked, never to return.

Because she wanted to. Even today, those four words added up to the clearest reason she could remember.

It took at least twenty minutes to get to the right place, another fifteen to find the road and a further five to climb to the top of a steep hill where the industrial estate was situated. It was a lot newer than hers. Long detached units that looked like overgrown garden sheds, separate car bays outside each one, huge shuttered doors. Taking only the smallest glances left and right, Adams headed for unit 51, the address on Yoshimoto's business card.

She found the car easily. The surrounding units were silent and, apart from the odd forklift truck, no other vehicles went by. The hairs on the back of her neck stood to attention. Every step was filled with hesitation as she approached the BMW, the car key hidden in her hand, waiting to hear the alarm at any moment. When it went off, Adams' minuscule plan was to grab the doll, run back down the hill as fast as her legs could carry her and hope that someone thought it was a false alarm. She had long dismissed any thoughts of CCTV, or of being caught in the act of stealing. The only thought on her mind was Sayaka.

She ran her fingers across the smooth, black boot. No alarm. She pushed the key into the lock, turned it slowly as she dared, heard the click as metal rubbed against metal. No alarm. She lifted the boot above her head, aware of every slow creak. When it was fully open and nothing happened, she was assailed by another, more recent memory: Mr. Yoshimoto knocking back the cloudy fizz of Alka Seltzer and looking at her, grateful as a dog receiving a bone. He'd been sick hadn't he? Maybe even sick enough to hurry back to work without setting his car alarm?

Adams was just reaching for the blue dustsheet when the man behind her spoke.

'What d'you think you're doin'?'

She turned. The security guard was wearing the usual beige shirt with matching creased trousers and brown shoes shined to a mirror finish. He had a walkie-talkie and a cloth badge that told everyone his occupation, but thankfully, no gun. He was burly, black, and not bad looking either. Adams kept her face down, embarrassed.

'Mr. Yoshimoto…'

'Mr... who?'

The guard was still frowning; even so, she wanted to hug him, plant a big smacker right on his juicy lips. The two words he'd spoken might as well have been *life* and *line*.

'Kenishi Yoshimoto. My boyfriend. He wanted me to get something out of his car for him...' She waited a moment, looked into his eyes, and raised her freshly cut keys.

'... Even gave me these...'

The burly guard stared, then made a rapid decision.

'Come inside a minute, let's sort this...'

'But...'

'Let's go...'

She put a hand on the boot, heart wrenching in fear, knowing that she was heading for more trouble than she'd ever been involved in, when a crackle of static roared abruptly from behind her. Her heart leapt once more. When she turned back to face him, he was glaring into the receiver of his walkie-talkie, one hand on his hip like a cowboy.

'Zero-one, zero-one.'

More static, before a voice emerged from deep within the crackles like a woodsman fighting through dense forest.

'Zero-one, this is Zero-five; could you report immediately to the Grey room?'

He looked at her balefully when he replied, but she could tell she was saved; the anger in his eyes was a clear indication.

'On way, Zero-five; over and out.'

'Over and out.'

He put the walkie-talkie back on his waist belt.

'I'll be checkin' up on you,' the man snarled.

He left Adams holding the boot high above her head, whispering a prayer between shallow sips of breath.

Hefting Sayaka under one arm, Adams got on the first bus that arrived. It would take her as far as East Acton underground station. From there she would catch the Central line back to her workshop. Once upstairs on the old Routemaster, Adams removed the dustsheet from the doll, positioned her limbs so that she could sit upright, and turned her head to the left so that Sayaka could look out of the window. Yes, people were staring, but it was a free country, wasn't it? They were just as entitled to stare as she was to ride the bus with a mannequin for a friend. She wasn't going to be ashamed, and if people thought this was strange behaviour, well that was up to them. She even found the courage to put an arm around Sayaka as the conductor warily approached. Adams looked up into his craggy face, beamed her cheeriest smile, and asked for two to East Acton please.

THE LAST WORD...

If I'm really honest, I suppose I got into the idea of dark short stories from the very first movies I saw, way back when I was a little kid. My parents had just moved into their first real home together, a two bedroom house in the suburbs of London. My dad was one of those men who loved all the materialistic trappings that were available in the seventies, so the cinecamera and projector he bought were no doubt seen as 'essential items'. He'd set up the projector in the living room and there (overriding the complaints of my mum) we would watch a succession of horror movies, from feature lengths about men being bitten by and then being turned into snakes, to old black and whites where a slow-moving yet purposeful monster stalked an innocent and beautiful maiden. I have to confess, I loved those films. From then on, horror was my stable celluloid diet, helped I think, by the fact that we were just entering the 80s, the era of the stalk n' slash movie. From Freddy, to Jason, to Michael Myers, I overdosed on them all. The first time I saw *Alien* was in book form. I read the blurb over and over, unable to understand what it was talking about (I must have been five or six at the time) and until I saw the film I thought that most of the action took place on a boat. By the age of ten, I was reading everything I could get my hands on, but sci-fi and horror had truly claimed me. *Star Wars, Lord of the Rings, Alien* and a host of other films and books (if I saw the film there was no question that I would read the book) fired my imagination.

There was a lot of good stuff on TV too, and a great deal more drama than there is today. One of the programmes I'd watch religiously was *Tales of the Unexpected*. Every weekend my parents would take my brother and myself from the suburbs to Harlesden, where we were deposited in the charge of my Gran Gran, Ms. Altina Denny. There, all three of us would sit in front of the telly waiting for that strange music and the woman doing her 'funny dance', as my Gran Gran called it. There was also *Hammer House of Horror*, another programme made up of a series of short, quirky films that explored the darker side of human nature. By my early teens, an English teacher called Jane Youlton set off a creative spark that, unknown to anyone at the time, never stopped burning. As well as introducing me to Chester Himes, who no doubt helped influence my later novels, she also introduced me to *Kiss Kiss* – Roald Dahl's collection of short stories with twists in their tails.

★

For a long time I did nothing with these creative inputs, although *Kiss Kiss* was a book that never left my memory. I loved it – in fact, if I remember correctly, the whole class loved it. I was writing at the time, but mainly as a hobby. I definitely never saw myself as a writer. My stuff was contemporary, dealing with everyday life in my area – a forerunner of what I was to write later. I kept it to myself, apart from showing it to my English teacher and my mother. I never told my friends what I was up to.

I didn't start writing seriously until my 21st birthday and I didn't start on short stories until I'd finished *The Scholar*. I wrote a collection called *West Side Stories,* taken from *The Scholar* subtitle, just because I was too lazy to write another novel but was keen not to stop altogether. My first piece, *What Goes Around*, involved a crackhead called Boney. I found myself desperately trying to emulate the twist device I'd seen used to such devastating effect in Roald Dahl stories such as 'Royal Jelly' and my all time favourite, 'Lamb to the Slaughter'. Other stories, like Langston Hughes' 'Home', from his collection *The Ways of White Folks* further cemented my ambitions. My goal was to write ten, purely for practice. I ended up with fifty. Eight years later only one of those ten original pieces made it into this particular collection – but I won't say which. I found short stories an entirely different form to novels, one that had an addictive appeal. Soon I was being asked to supply pieces on commission. My first, a Greenside tale for those who missed the characters, was selected for a collection called *Disco 2000*, the follow up to the hugely successful *Disco Biscuits*, which had sold 50,000 copies. That story never made this book, although there are five other previously published stories within this collection.

Music for the Off-Key is a collection of surreal short stories using Black people as the main characters. The title stems from an interesting bit of London slang – someone or something that is off-key means that they or it is a little bit crazy, a little bit weird. *Music for the Off-Key* means that these are stories written for those who like their fiction on the surreal side. Too often I feel, as Black writers in the UK, we are trapped within the walls of three subjects – the Windrush Novel, the Gangster Novel and the I'm-not-really-Black novel – particularly when we are dealing with mainstream publishing houses. I have nothing against the topics, their authors, or mainstream publishing houses, but the writers I admire – Chester Himes, Rupert Thomson, Langston Hughes, Iain Banks, Paul Auster – switch subjects as and when they please, keeping their audience guessing and, I suspect, themselves. This lack of vision means that Black writing in the UK has ground to an uncertain creative halt. Writers who don't wish to cover the above subjects are left out in the cold. White writers try and ape, 'the Black experience', as if all we know is how to be poor and immigrant. Wherever I go I see that there are more writers and styles than ever, but if we are constantly being asked to regurgitate the same old stories for the same old readers, we won't have anything near an explosive scene. At the moment, what we have amounts to nothing more than a damp squib.

I've always thought that there's no point being an artist if you're not going to push boundaries with your art. I hope I've managed to achieve that aim with this collection.

Courttia Newland
West London 2004
www.telltales.co.uk 'Live to Tell the Tale; Tell the Tale to Live.'

ABOUT THE AUTHOR

Courttia Newland is the author of three critically acclaimed novels, *The Scholar*, *Society Within* and *Snakeskin*. He has co-edited *IC3: The Penguin Book of New Black Writing in Britain* and is a co-founder of the Tell Tales collective, a short story initiative. His own short stories been published in many anthologies and several of his plays have been performed in venues all over London, including *The Far Side* (Tricycle), *Mother's Day* (Lyric, Hammersmith) and *B is 4 Black* (Oval House). A novella, *The Dying Wish* (Abacus) was published in 2006 as part of the Quick Reads Series and his first radio play, Hands, will be broadcast on BBC radio 4 in April of the same year. You can visit his website at www.courttianewland.com.

Earlier versions of these stories have appeared in the following publications:

Complexion…, *Vintage New Writers 8*, February 1999.
The Great White Hate, *Afrobeat*, October 1999
His Healing Hands, *Rites of Spring*, February 1999
Suicide Note, *Time Out London Shorts* October 2000
Sound of the Drums, *England Calling*, October 2001
Flight of Freedom, *Freedom One Day*, June 2002

Dark, compelling, twisted and grim in all the best ways possible, these stories turn us into, in Forster's phrase, 'the shock-headed public gaping round the campfire'. With the texture of urban folktale, the monsters they feature crawl from sexual obsession, prejudice, and other forms of hate. 'Sound of the Drums' is a terrifying tale of jealousy and self-absorption set in a muddy field lit by strobe and bonfire. Ancient terrors re-appear amongst concrete, below underpasses, in raves, scratching at the tenth-floor windows of tower blocks. This is powerful, intense, and engaging writing.

Niall Griffiths, author of Wreckage

Fantasy, desire and betrayal; just some of the themes in Courttia Newland's intriguing debut collection of short stories, *Music for the Off Key*. Newland has often been lauded for his ability to portray the lives of ordinary black people in a way that shuns the stereotypical. Here we are presented with 12 distinct characters, all rooted in the Black British experience and all representing just how broad that experience can be.

Meet Welling, the forty something artist whose penchant for relationships with vulnerable young girls pushes him into signing an irreversible life-threatening contract. Or meet Marcus Jennings, whose annoying itch magically develops into the means for his escape from his stifling inner-city environment. In 'Gold' Laramie the vagrant, recklessly betrays the naïve and trusting Blaine, and in doing so misses out on perhaps his last chance of love and security.

Newland's prose has a fluidity and resonance rarely seen in writing about inner-city life. With a great ear for both dialogue and description he entices us into a world where ordinary living provides the background for extraordinary experiences. It's a credit to Newland's storytelling that many of the stories straddle an uncertain line between the actual and the magical, and are all the more absorbing for it. Never judgemental and certainly never apologetic, Newland skilfully challenges modern day perceptions of what it means to be black in Britain.

A long awaited collection from an outstanding storyteller, *Music for the Off Key* is a memorable celebration of the surreal nature of everyday life

Andrea Enisuoh, New Nation

Courttia Newland is a man who makes things happen, a leading figure in his generation of writers. His plays and stories pack a powerful punch and reach parts of the community other writers don't reach.

Maggie Gee, author of The White Family

Go to www.peepaltreepress.com to find twenty-one other collections of short stories amongst almost two hundred titles in print – the very best of Caribbean and Black British writing.

All Peepal Tree books should be available through your local bookseller, though you are even more welcome to place orders direct with us on the Peepal Tree website and on-line bookstore. You can also order direct by phone or in writing.

Peepal Tree sends out regular e-mail information about new books and special offers. We also produce a twice-yearly stock catalogue, and new and forthcoming titles catalalogue to keep you up to date with what's coming up. Contact us to join our mailing list.

You can contact Peepal Tree at:

> 17 King's Avenue
> Leeds LS6 1QS
> United Kingdom
>
> e-mail info@peepaltreepress.com
> tel: 44 (0)113 245 1703
> website: www.peepaltreepress.com